Andy Shepherd

The Ultimate Guide to

GROWING DRAGONS

Illustrated by Sara Ogilvie

Piccadilly
PRESS

First published in Great Britain in 2022 by
PICCADILLY PRESS
4th Floor, Victoria House, Bloomsbury Square
London WC1B 4DA
Owned by Bonnier Books
Sveavägen 56, Stockholm, Sweden
www.piccadillypress.co.uk

A CIP catalogue record for this book is available from the British Library.

ISBN: 978-1-80078-315-7
Signed edition ISBN: 978-1-80078-546-5
Also available as an ebook and in audio

1 3 5 7 9 10 8 6 4 2

Typeset by Emily Bornoff
Printed and bound in Great Britain by Clays Ltd, Elcograf S.p.A.

Piccadilly Press is an imprint of Bonnier Books UK
www.bonnierbooks.co.uk

For Ian, Ben and Jonas,
who lift me as high as any dragon

And for all you wonderful dragon desperados –
thank you for giving the dragons a home!

THE ULTIMATE GUIDE TO GROWING DRAGONS

CONTENTS

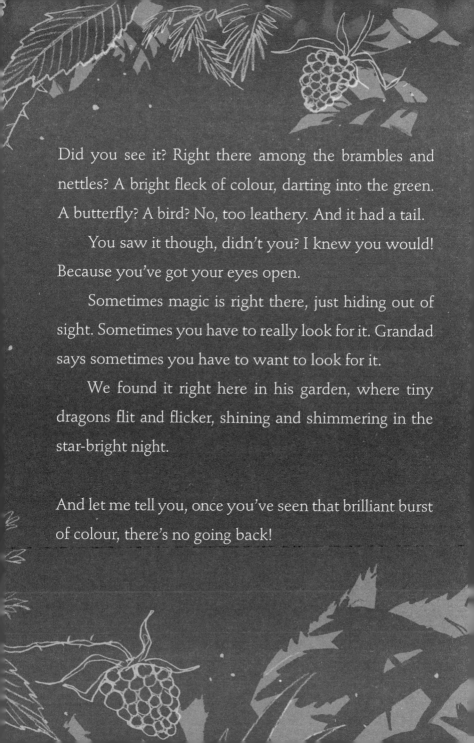

Did you see it? Right there among the brambles and nettles? A bright fleck of colour, darting into the green. A butterfly? A bird? No, too leathery. And it had a tail.

You saw it though, didn't you? I knew you would! Because you've got your eyes open.

Sometimes magic is right there, just hiding out of sight. Sometimes you have to really look for it. Grandad says sometimes you have to want to look for it.

We found it right here in his garden, where tiny dragons flit and flicker, shining and shimmering in the star-bright night.

And let me tell you, once you've seen that brilliant burst of colour, there's no going back!

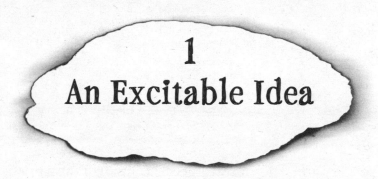

1
An Excitable Idea

So, are you ready? Ready to grow a dragon?

The answer to that question is NO. You're not ready. Because honestly, you're never really ready for a dragon. I know I wasn't when Flicker first arrived.

Of course, if you've followed the story so far – and it's been quite a ride! – you'll be better prepared than most, and that's good. But honestly, if you're new to all this, don't worry. Just keep your eyes open and some oven gloves and water pistols handy and you'll be fine.

Anyway, as some of you might remember, I'm known as the Grand High DragonMaster.

What's that?

Fine.

You're right. The closest I get to claiming that name is when Ted calls me Grand High PongMaster. Just call me Tomas then.

The first thing you should know about me is that I get ideas. All the time. And the biggest ones often come barging into my room just as I'm about to fall asleep.

They don't seem to care about being polite and waiting until I'm sitting somewhere sensible with a pen and a piece of paper. This idea bounced on my bed till I was properly awake. And because it was so big it was like having an elephant and a gerbil on the same trampoline, with me being the gerbil, almost boinging across the room. It even woke up Zing, who immediately started zooming around.

Zing is a pretty excitable dragon and when he zips about he charges up with electricity and can zap from one place to another. You never know where he might pop up, which is not exactly relaxing. So with an excitable dragon and an excitable idea on the loose, I knew I wasn't going to get any sleep.

I switched on my rocket lamp and grabbed a notebook. The first page only had a doodle of Mr Firth drinking a cup of coffee. You might think that a picture of your teacher having a drink was a pretty weird and boring thing to draw. Until I tell you my dragon Flicker had just done a poo in it! That was back when Flicker was small enough to fly round my classroom. Now anytime Mr Firth annoys me, I just remember that day.

I seized the idea zooming round my room with Zing and caught it in my book. And this was it: a plan to write everything down EVERYTHING I KNOW ABOUT GROWING DRAGONS.

All the things it would have been good to know back at the start, in one easy-to-read and easy-to-find place.

Of course, what I didn't know when I started this guide was just how much I still had to learn!

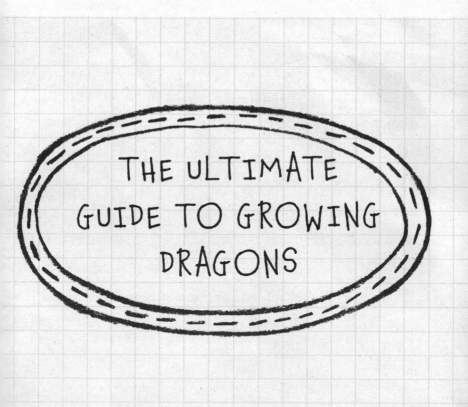

THE ULTIMATE GUIDE TO GROWING DRAGONS

THE BIG SECRET

Let's start with the basics.

I bet, like me, you thought that dragons come from eggs like this one.

They may be found
on beaches or
in caves or hidden on
mountaintops and vary
in size and colour.

Sea dragon egg – soft shell
with blue and green ripples
        like sunlight on the sea.

**Mountain
dragon egg** –
glints red and
gold like the sun
at sunrise.

Sand dragon egg
– small (size of your
thumbnail), can withstand
extreme heat and cold.

Forest dragon egg –
mottled emerald green and
brown, prickly surface
a bit like a conker case.

Well, we were kind of right, because some do come from eggs.

But I discovered a secret.

(You can keep secrets, right? I probably should have checked that before I let you read this. I know I told Ted, Kat and Kai, and Grandad, and I did blurt it out to Aura, oh and there's . . . never mind. I'm not talking about me. Anyway, they're all part of the superhero squad now. And you can be too. But first I absolutely need to know that you'll keep this secret to yourself. OK?)

So here goes — here's what you might not have heard from all the dragon stories you've read before.

SOME DRAGONS GROW ON TREES!

Yup! On a really special tree called a dragon-fruit tree.

And I bet I can guess your next question — where do I find myself one of these dragon trees?

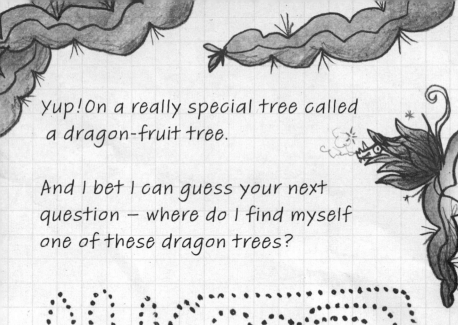

You want a map? Sorry but it doesn't work like that. There's no '**you are here**', '**dragon is here**'. You just have to keep your eyes open.

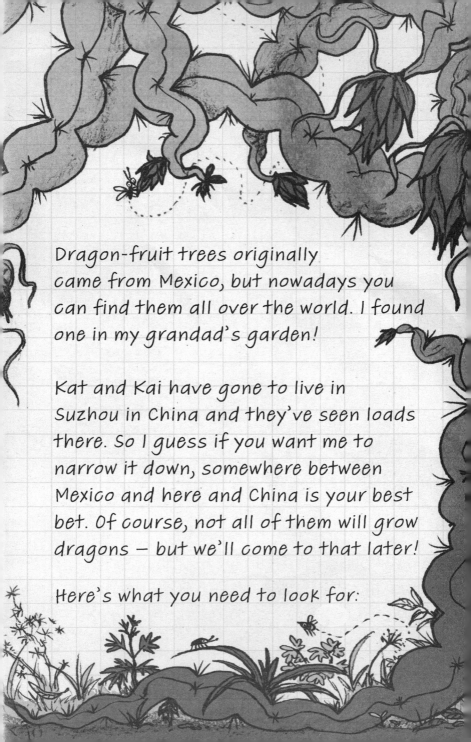

Dragon-fruit trees originally came from Mexico, but nowadays you can find them all over the world. I found one in my grandad's garden!

Kat and Kai have gone to live in Suzhou in China and they've seen loads there. So I guess if you want me to narrow it down, somewhere between Mexico and here and China is your best bet. Of course, not all of them will grow dragons — but we'll come to that later!

Here's what you need to look for:

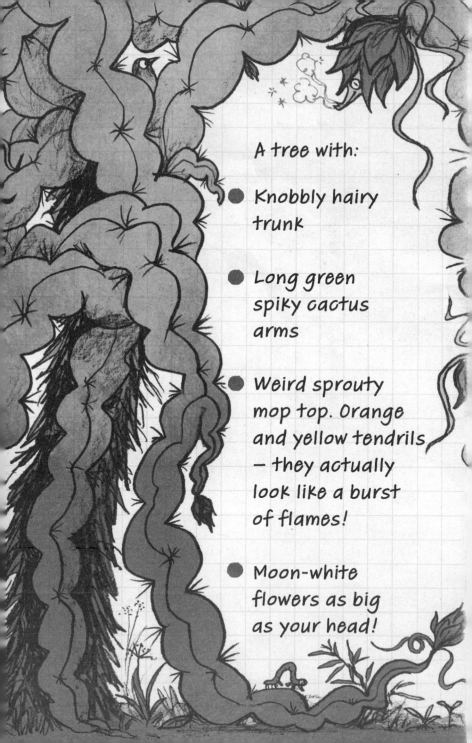

A tree with:

- Knobbly hairy trunk

- Long green spiky cactus arms

- Weird sprouty mop top. Orange and yellow tendrils — they actually look like a burst of flames!

- Moon-white flowers as big as your head!

TOP TIP 1: If you want to see the flowers you'll need to set up camp. Because they ONLY bloom at night.

TOP TIP 2: Don't borrow your grandparents' tent — we did and it smelled of feet and collapsed.

After the tendrils have grown and the moon-white flowers have bloomed, the fruit will start to grow.

BE PATIENT!

Wait for the fruit to turn red and ripe. Don't pick them before that, because the dragons might not be ready. Once the fruit starts to glow you know it's nearly time to meet your dragon. The fruit will fall — onto the ground or into your hand — when it's time for it to burst. Some of us wonder if the dragons choose whose hand their fruit will drop into.

If Ted and Sunny are anything to go by, dragons do seem to seek out someone a bit like them.

I was pretty pleased with all that writing. It'd taken ages, and by the time I put my pen down my hand was aching and Zing had fallen asleep on my bed.

I was so excited to tell the rest of the superhero squad about my big idea that I sent a group message to them all.

Then I crawled under the covers and thankfully no more ideas barged in to wake me up again till morning – when my little sister Lolli woke me up with my own personal drum roll.

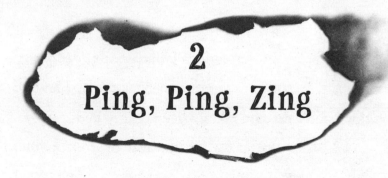

2
Ping, Ping, Zing

'Ping ping ping!' Lolli cried as the drum rolling came to an end.

I peered blearily over the quilt, which I'd been using to shield my ears.

'Your 'puter's going ping ping PING!' she said, pointing at the laptop on my desk. And then giggled as Zing zapped out from under the bed and appeared on my head just as another PING sounded.

'Zing go ping,' she said. And then added with glee, 'Zing go ping, ring a ding ding, shiny little wing, funny little fing. Sing a sing sing. ZING!'

I grinned. Ever since Dad had started teaching her

little songs on the keyboard, Lolli had decided to go hunting for rhymes. She got very jiggly when a word was especially 'rhymy-whymy'.

She had also got very cross at oranges. Until Mum told her 'orange' rhymed with 'sporange', which is part of a fern apparently. Although Lolli decided a sporange was actually a sponge who'd swallowed an orange.

Which made her feel sorry for oranges and like them all over again.

While Lolli skipped out and headed downstairs, I went over and woke up the computer screen. The superhero squad had replied!

Ted
Epic idea, Pongmaster!

Liam
Sounds cool. Here's me next to a wall. This has got to be the most boring place to come on holiday! YAWNNNNNN.

Kat and Kai

We're in! Sorry got to run now. We're all going to Tiger Hill to explore. Will check in later.

'Exploring' and 'Tiger Hill' sounded pretty amazing. I did some quick calculating. It was about two o'clock in Suzhou, and if they were going exploring it could be hours before the twins were back online. Ever since Kat and Kai had moved to China, I'd been doing a lot of maths, trying to work out time differences. And with Aura away in Mexico visiting our friend Arturo, I had even more to do. With some of the superhero squad seven hours ahead and another member six hours behind, my brain was on the verge of exploding!

It was just as well that Liam had only ventured as far as Suffolk for the summer holidays, and although Ted was in Spain, that was only an hour ahead.

19

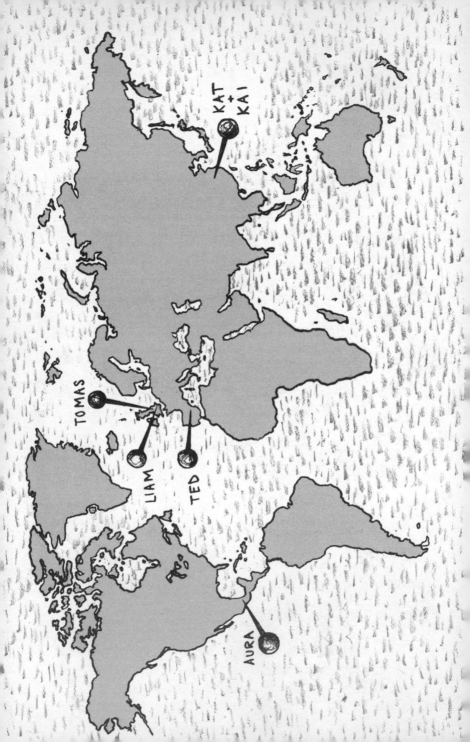

Aura

Hola, Tomas!

An Ultimate Guide to Growing Dragons! With everything we've found out!! That's a brilliant idea!!!!

Aura likes exclamation marks. Her emails jump into my room feet together, arms flapping, ready to shout 'BOO!'; a whirlwind of words just like real-life Aura.

Aura continued . . .

I've already got something we can put in. You know how we found out that dragon-fruit trees don't just grow straight out of the ground like the tree in your grandad's garden? Some of them grow on other trees. Well, I've seen one! Remember I told you about Arely, Arturo's great-niece? She has one growing on a tree in her garden. It gets its food and drink from the air and rain. Sometimes they're really hard to spot because they grow so high up in the canopy. I think it's so they can hide from danger like our dragons do!

Here's a picture! We should put that in the guide. And we should add a top tip: don't forget to look up sometimes, because you never know what you're missing.

Also, meet Quetzalcoatl!!!

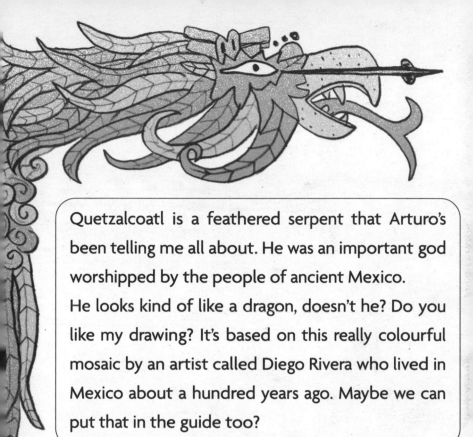

Quetzalcoatl is a feathered serpent that Arturo's been telling me all about. He was an important god worshipped by the people of ancient Mexico.

He looks kind of like a dragon, doesn't he? Do you like my drawing? It's based on this really colourful mosaic by an artist called Diego Rivera who lived in Mexico about a hundred years ago. Maybe we can put that in the guide too?

I had to admit those were some brilliant things to include. Aura was seeing so much cool stuff. I wished I had so many exciting new things to share. But at least I knew all about looking after the tree, so I decided to focus on that next.

HOW TO LOOK AFTER YOUR TREE!

Have you ever been given a packet of seeds and tried to grow a carrot or a sunflower?

You press a hole in the soil, pop in the seed, give it a bit of water and stick it somewhere warm. And before you know it there's a little shoot of green. And if you're careful you might even end up with a prize-winning flower or what Grandad calls his VIPs (Vegetable Impersonator Produce). You know the kind of thing — a pumpkin that looks like the prime minister or a runner bean who you're sure you saw score the winning goal of a match.

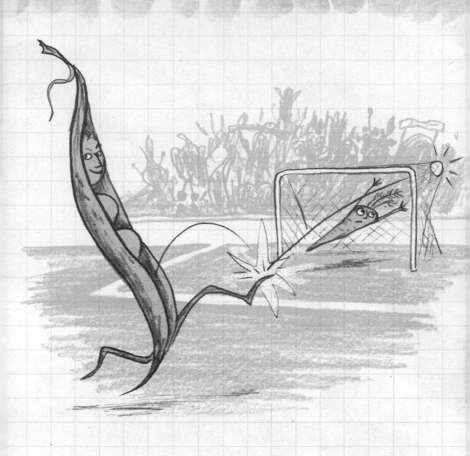

Well, growing dragons isn't like that
AT ALL.

For a start, the dragon-fruit tree
they grow on is a bit fussy (like Lolli,
who licks the jam out of her roly-poly
pudding and leaves the rest).

THINGS DRAGON-FRUIT TREES DO NOT LIKE:

- Too much water. Dragon-fruit trees are cacti and they don't like getting their feet wet. I learned that from Chouko Sato and she's been working at the Botanic Garden for years and years so she knows what she's talking about.

● Being too cold. Ours was protected from the worst wintery weather by what Grandad calls the bongleweed, that had grown up around it. Now we've cleared that away we have to be a bit careful. So we put lots of mulch on the soil to protect its roots. And if it's really cold we have a special blanket to keep it warm and a little shelter that Grandad made to put round it as a windbreak.

THINGS DRAGON-FRUIT TREES LIKE:

● Being talked to or sung to. Grandad's neighbour, Jim, says all plants like this. Personally I think it might depend on who's doing the singing. Once I played 'Three Blind

Mice' on my ukulele to the seedling I was looking after, but if anything it made it shrivel up more. So proceed with caution — and maybe practise on a piece of lettuce first.

- Ash — dragon-fruit trees love this just as much as dragons do. (More on how to use ash to train your dragon later. You need to grow one first!) Sprinkle five teaspoonfuls per day around the roots.

Chocolate: Ted says chocolate is the answer to everything — and it turns out dragon-fruit trees agree! They LOVE chocolate. I spent ages trying and failing to grow the dragon-fruit tree seedlings that I was looking after and all along they just wanted a nice big dollop of chocolate. Like Ted does ninety-two per cent of the time. (The other eight per cent he wants crisps.)

BUT before you rush out and throw your last chocolate bar at the garden, it's cocoa mulch you need. Which is more of a grainy bean mash than a creamy caramel treat! It 'keeps the moisture in and the weeds out,' Grandad says.

So I'm sorry if, like Lolli, you were imagining chocolate bars lying all over the garden! Ever since she made that mistake, I've been dreaming about a tree that grows chocolate bars and sweets!

If you look after your tree well, you can expect four or five crops of fruit a year. THAT'S A LOT OF DRAGONS!

3
A Wise Teddy

After breakfast, Mum, who's a vet and likes to bring her work home with her, needed an extra pair of hands to help clean out the rabbits, hamsters, gerbils and tarantulas she was looking after – yes, you heard right, that's multiple tarantulas! Personally, Itsy and Bitsy have helped me get over the whole being-alarmed-by-spiders thing, but Ted still refuses to go into our lounge, where Mum's put their vivarium. Anyway, it turned out she probably needed at least ten extra pairs of hands, because it was the middle of the afternoon by the time I got over to Nana and Grandad's house. I found Grandad in his shed, planting seeds into tiny pots of earth. He

gently patted each one and gave it a little drink before moving onto the next. He tucked them in as carefully as he tucked us into bed.

I perched on the stool and told him all about my big idea.

'Sounds like you've got yourself a plan there, Chipstick. Between your superhero squad and Elvi and Arturo, you've got all sorts of know-how.'

'We had to hunt pretty hard to find it all,' I said, thinking of the digging we'd had to do to find Elvi's diaries and Arturo's letters. 'It'd be a lot easier to have it all in one place.'

Grandad chuckled. 'You're right there. It certainly kept you amused.'

I couldn't help smiling as I thought of Elvi and her best friend Arturo. Elvi was Aura's grandmother, her amma, and she'd lived in Nana and Grandad's house before they had. She and Arturo might not have made it easy for us, but without Elvi growing her dragon-fruit tree from a seed, we'd never have grown dragons.

I showed him what I'd written about dragon-fruit trees. He studied it carefully, then took a pencil from the little pot with the carved dragon on and handed it to me.

'How about putting in something about the legend of the dragon fruit?' he said. He reached up and pulled down a dusty book from the shelf above our heads – one of Elvi's old ones. The title *A World of Plants* was half covered by a muddy handprint. He let the book fall open, scattering dust and startling an earwig. Flicking past the page with Elvi's name on it, he carried on until he got to the one about the dragon-fruit tree.

The encyclopedia hadn't told us anything about the dragons, but it did have one little bit about the legend of the fruit.

'How about you start with this? And then,' Grandad continued, 'you can add in the other things you found along the way.'

'But do you think anyone'll want to read about the history?' I asked, pausing to rub out my first attempt at a swirly capital 'L' for the title. 'Won't people just want to know how to grow dragons? I mean, I've already explained about how to look after the tree. I'm not sure anyone'll care about what happened years ago.'

'I'm not so sure about that,' Grandad said. 'It's like that famous Teddy said, "The more you know about the past, the better prepared you are for the future."'

'A teddy bear said that?'

Grandad's eyes twinkled. 'Teddy Roosevelt,' he said with a grin. 'I'll let you find out who he was.'

I began to copy what was written in the encyclopedia carefully into my notebook and then immediately wanted to cross it all out. Whoever had written this clearly had no idea about dragons if the only word they could use to describe them was 'monstrous'.

THE LEGEND OF THE DRAGON FRUIT

Legend has it that dragon fruit were created millennia ago from the fierce and fiery breath of monstrous dragons. In terrible battles when a dragon breathed its last breath, amid the dying flame a fruit would appear. The fruit was presented to the emperor as a symbol of power and victory over the slain dragon. It was a prized treasure that brought great reward and as such many people sought out dragons to vanquish to gain that favour and wealth.

WRONG!

Just so we're clear, the legend was all wrong. We'd worked that out already. Well, Kat had. She'd remembered what Miss Logan had said about legends and how they sometimes got altered over time.

So do you remember what I said earlier about not all dragon-fruit trees growing dragons? Well, here's why that is.

What if, Kat wondered, it's not that the dragons breathed *out* the fruit, but that they breathed *on* it and that's what turned a normal fruit into an active one – one whose seeds grow into a tree that hatches dragons? With that one question, everything had changed.

Introducing . . . ACTIVATOR DRAGONS!

ACTIVATOR DRAGONS

Activator dragons are super-rare, which is probably just as well because they are super-powerful. We learned that from Maxi, Liam's dragon. He's an activator dragon whose breath can super-size a marrow so it's big enough to ride like a rodeo bull. He also activated the fruit on the dragon-fruit tree Liam found in the botanic garden.

We later learned from Elvi and Arturo's letters how dangerous activator dragons could be. Arturo told Elvi about this rival to the emperor of the Hidden Dragon City who had got greedy and kept an activator dragon hostage.

'It grew fast and it grew big. And the green flames that spurted from its belly were too powerful. They razed the land, annihilating the crops and trees, and burned the great city to dust.'

So, whatever you do, don't keep an activator dragon! Because if you do then it'll be more than the odd dragon poo that explodes — it could be your whole town!

You have been warned!

What's the difference between an active dragon fruit and a non-active one? On the outside, nothing; on the inside, everything! So you'll have to wait and see — just keep your eyes wide open!

Normal dragon fruit

- Tasty refreshing snack.
- Won't grow dragons.

Active dragon fruit

- Breathed on by an activator dragon.
- Has seeds that grow into a tree that hatches dragons.

4
Time to Watch the Show

Now that we were in touch with Arturo, I wondered if maybe there was even more he could tell us. I decided to message Aura to get her to ask him. While I was doing that, Grandad lifted the lid on his secret stash of goodies and held it out to me. The shed instantly filled with the sweet smell of Nana's jammy tarts and ginger biscuits.

But before I could unstick one of the jam tarts there was a loud bang on the window and we spun round just in time to see a flash of bright orange disappearing from view.

Grandad winced. 'Bet that hurt,' he said. 'I thought it wouldn't be long till the next crop started bursting out of their fruits. Looks like that one's learned its first lesson about windows.'

I jumped up and hurried outside, scanning the ground to see if the little dragon who had just crashed into the glass had done itself some serious damage. But there was no sign of it. There was only Tomtom, our grumpy ginger cat, stalking away towards the house. He'd taken to eating breakfast at ours and then turning up at Nana and Grandad's for second breakfast, elevenses, lunch and dinner, before curling up in Nana's flower beds for a nap until it was time to come back home for bonus snack and late tea. Move over, Six Dinner Sid, the cat from Lolli's story book who ate multiple meals, and make way for Ten Tea Tomtom! I hunted round some more, but with no sign of a dazed dragon I had to hope it had simply flown off a bit stunned.

Grandad grinned. 'Time to watch the show, hey, Chipstick?'

I nodded eagerly and we headed towards the

tree. Its sprouting cactus arms reached out to us as we approached and my eyes lit up as I saw a couple of fruits already glowing. Seeing dragons emerge from the red ripe dragon fruits certainly beat picking slugs off lettuces. Which is what we had been planning to do!

Let me tell you, the first time you see a dragon bursting out of a dragon fruit your whole world lights up. It's like turning up the contrast on your TV and everything getting brighter. And it never dims, however many times you see it happen.

Of course, when I found the dragon-fruit tree in Grandad's garden, I didn't even know what it was. But I took one of the fruits home and typed in 'spiky fruit' on my computer and there it was: the pitaya, also known as a dragon fruit. Obviously back then I had no idea there was actually a dragon growing inside, so when something burst out of it in the middle of the night and landed behind my beanbag, I freaked myself out imagining it was some kind of mutant maggot!

But then I saw Flicker. This little ruby shimmering dragon. And BAM the world lit up, as bright as his scales. And that was it, the moment my life changed forever. Because once you grow a dragon you have a friend for life.

Since then there have been all sorts of dragons growing on our tree.

Dragons that breathe ice, like Kat's dragon Crystal, and dragons who are masters of camouflage, like Kai's Dodger. Dragons like Liam's Maxi who can super-size things, and dragons that fill the sky with song like Tinkle, Lolli's dragon. Even dragons like Ted's Sunny, who shine like the sun and, let's face it, eat anything and everything in sight. And although our dragons are fully-grown now and spend time away from us, there are still plenty of new dragons bursting from the fruits.

We've seen corkscrew-tailed drilling dragons and dragons that squirt slime, tiny bee dragons and dragons like Aura's dragon Rosebud with her petal-shaped

wings and green gas that makes us giggle. And of course zapping sparky ones like Zing, the little dragon whose fruit I nearly squashed and who flew straight at my face when he burst out. He's been keeping me company – and on my toes – ever since.

I shuffled closer to Grandad on the bench and we both grinned as we waited to see what kinds of dragons there would be this time and what abilities they might have – though that wasn't always immediately clear.

'I should do a fact file on each dragon and put them in the guide,' I said.

'Great idea, Chipstick,' Grandad agreed. 'Better sharpen your pencil, because there are about to be a whole lot more!'

FLICKER

Type: Weather dragon

Physical characteristics: Ruby-red scales, diamond eyes, arrowhead tail, spines, horns (one longer than the other), scalloped glittery wings, sharp claws (three at the front and one at the back of each foot).

Diet: Favourite food is broccoli, but he will eat most plants.

Special skills: Can conjure storms, wind, rain, lightning. Can change colour depending on mood. Turquoise scales mean he's calm. Bright orange and he's alarmed and ready for action. And if he's really happy it'll be like looking through a kaleidoscope!

~~**Personality**~~ **Dragonality:** Full of bright ideas. Very loyal.

Warning: If you look into his diamond eyes he can see right into the heart of you. So if you're trying to hide the fact you ate the last doughnut, don't let him catch your eye. There's no fibbing near Flicker! Also – as with most dragons – watch out for exploding poos!

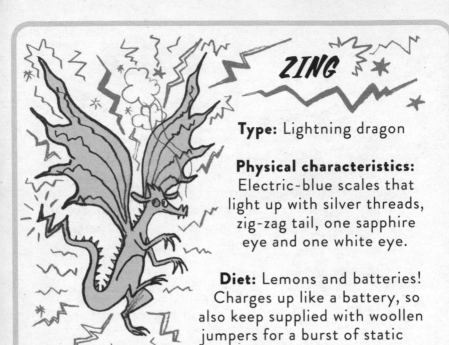

ZING

Type: Lightning dragon

Physical characteristics: Electric-blue scales that light up with silver threads, zig-zag tail, one sapphire eye and one white eye.

Diet: Lemons and batteries! Charges up like a battery, so also keep supplied with woollen jumpers for a burst of static electricity.

Special skills: Can belch lightning and teleport – 'zap' – from one place to another.

Dragonality: Curious, playful, energetic

Warning: If you see a lightning bolt flash across his white eye, you know he's about to zap out of sight, only to reappear who knows where!
Can give you a mild static shock that will make your hair stand on end.

5
The Star Dragon

The first dragon we saw didn't stick around. It circled the tree a few times, shaking the sticky pulp from its barbed tail, and then shot off up into the sky. But others stayed for a bite to eat before they headed off on their journey, guided by the North Star.

THE NORTH STAR
ALSO CALLED: POLE STAR, POLARIS

This star guides the dragons
to their home in the far north.

Take note — on cloudy nights any
dragons you grow might stick around
for longer!

WHERE DRAGONS AND STARS MEET

We've soared with the dragons on star-
bright nights, but I never knew a dragon
was shining down on us until I found a
book in the library about astronomy.

Meet Draco the Dragon! Draco is a

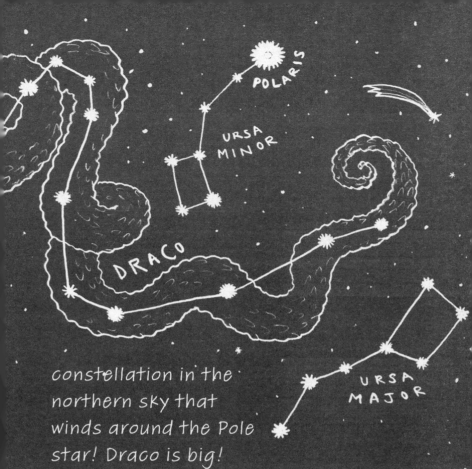

constellation in the
northern sky that
winds around the Pole
star! Draco is big!

   On a dark night you can make
out two stars that make up the
dragon's head. Called Rastaban and
Eltanin, they're the eyes of the dragon
shining down.

   So all along the dragons have been
following Draco — the star dragon.

HOW TO SPOT POLARIS

You can see Polaris from anywhere
in the northern hemisphere. If you're
standing on the equator it'll be on the
horizon, and the further north you go,
the higher it rises in the sky, until at
the North Pole it's directly overhead.
You can find Polaris in the sky by
locating Ursa Major — also known as
the Plough or the Big Dipper. Imagine a
line going up from the two front stars
of the Plough. Continue tracing the line
outwards and the first bright star you
come to is Polaris.

If you're south of the equator you won't
see Polaris, but don't worry, your
dragons are guided by the constellation
called the Southern Cross — the Crux.
They know that by flying away from the

Southern Cross, they're heading north. When they pass the equator they will see Polaris to guide them on the rest of their long journey.

A long slender dragon with scales shining gold had homed in on Grandad's herbs. Luckily he didn't mind the devastation the dragons caused. He always factored in some losses to his planting.

'You planning on opening a greengrocer's?' Jim would ask with a raised eyebrow as he spotted the rows upon rows of newly sprouting flowers and vegetables housed in Grandad's greenhouse. And Grandad would give me a wink and simply say, 'Oh, you know those slugs, Jim. Appetites the size of dragons!'

It was just as well he did have more herbs growing, because the golden dragon had been joined by two smaller dragons, one with bright white scales and an orange tail and the other a glimmering aqua blue. I wondered if the orange-tailed dragon was the one who'd flown into the window. If it was, then I was relieved to see it looked fine, its little tail flicking back and forth happily as it devoured the tender leaves of Grandad's basil plant.

'Watch out!' Grandad chuckled, pulling me closer just as a cluster of tiny bee dragons zoomed past my head.

These dragons were little shiny jewels, each one a different colour, but all with orange wings. They were fast too and could do some pretty incredible stunt flying, with fancy loop-the-loops and even zipping about backwards!

I jumped off the bench, laughing as one of them got blown off course by a gust of wind and veered towards my head. I knew from experience that they had a fairly zappy sting on them, and although it probably wouldn't be on purpose, I didn't fancy being on the receiving end.

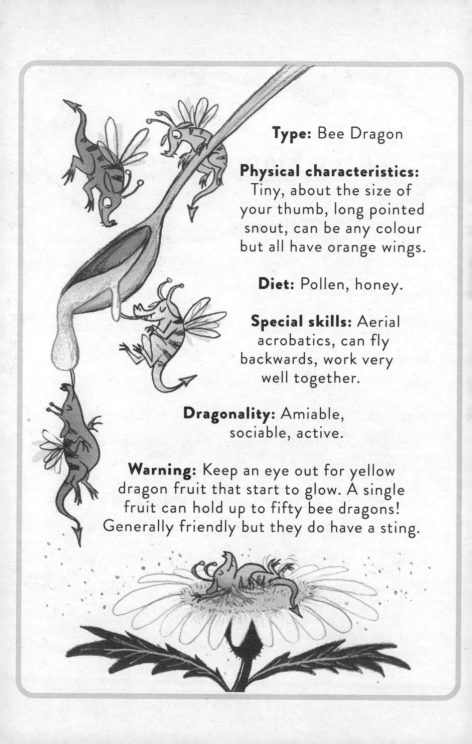

Type: Bee Dragon

Physical characteristics: Tiny, about the size of your thumb, long pointed snout, can be any colour but all have orange wings.

Diet: Pollen, honey.

Special skills: Aerial acrobatics, can fly backwards, work very well together.

Dragonality: Amiable, sociable, active.

Warning: Keep an eye out for yellow dragon fruit that start to glow. A single fruit can hold up to fifty bee dragons! Generally friendly but they do have a sting.

6
Furry Flapping Iglets

I headed over to the dragon-fruit tree to see how many more ripe fruits still hung on the branches. I counted fifteen! It looked like Grandad might need a bigger greenhouse before too long – there seemed to be more and more fruits growing with each new crop.

As I watched one of the fruits starting to glow, I heard a high-pitched screech. I turned to see Lolli skipping past the apple trees. She was wearing a huge furry hat with fluffy ear flaps that bounced as she skipped and what looked like one of Grandad's bobbly gardening jumpers. The sleeves were so big that they almost reached the ground, although not for long as she was flapping her arms on each skip.

I glanced back at the fruit, which had stopped glowing for the moment, then back at Lolli.

She squawked loudly, flapped around Grandad, who was loading up a wheelbarrow, then 'flew' over to me. She started opening and closing her mouth.

'Chick?' I ventured.

She nodded. 'I'm an iglet,' she declared.

I must have looked confused because she said it again more slowly and then, after a second or two added, 'That's a baby eagle.'

'I think you mean "eaglet",' I replied, finally understanding.

'That's what I said. An iglet.'

She plumped up her imaginary feathers proudly.

I nodded. 'I think the ears confused me,' I said. 'I'm not sure eaglets have big flappy ears.'

Lolli wrinkled her nose, her hands feeling the hat. 'Nana tucked them in,' she said crossly, 'but they fell

out.' She shrugged and stuck out her cheeks, then flapped off, ears and all.

When another fruit burst and a rather plump dragon with knobbly horns and a short stubby tail emerged, Lolli circled back.

She watched it nibbling at the bits of dragon-fruit skin stuck to its front leg. It unfurled its wings, which were spotted black and red like a ladybird's, and took off, landing on a nearby branch.

Lolli squeezed her face extra tight in concentration and flapped and flapped her sleeve wings. Then she paused and looked down at the ground. A frustrated breath burst out, leaving a little pout behind.

'Iglets can't fly till they're big,' she said.

I nodded.

'I want to be big,' she added quietly.

I thought of flying with Flicker and the feeling that whooshed up from my toes to my ears as we rocketed through the sky. Lolli had always been too small to ride on Tinkle when the rest of us flew away into the night.

I gave her furry ear a stroke and whispered, 'Two chocolate frogs says the next dragon is stripy like a zebra with sixteen heads, twenty-seven tails, no wings and can tap-dance.'

She giggled and grabbed my hand to shake on it before I could change my mind. Then she took up watch on the tree.

We didn't have to wait long. A fruit on one of the long cactus arms nearest the ground started bulging. A second later out popped a bright green dragon with just the one head and one spiny tail and, given that it managed to trip over that tail on its way to standing up, I guessed not enough coordination to tap-dance.

Lolli danced around gleefully, hand out for her froggy prize.

By teatime the garden had welcomed ten more little dragons. They darted around us, shimmering flecks of colour in the afternoon light. Some of the braver ones flew close, inspecting us with their bright little eyes. They seemed spurred on by Zing, who was clearly happy clinging to my back in between zipping around after them.

A tiny purple bee dragon with a pink band along its belly settled on Lolli's furry head and she tiptoed towards me, eyes sparkling, with her finger on her lips.

'When I said we have to keep the dragons under our hat I meant keep them secret,' I said, laughing. 'Not actually in your hat!'

I don't think I needed to worry though – this little

dragon was entirely happy up there. And when after
a few minutes she forgot and started skipping around
again it stayed happily nestled in the fur.

WHERE TO KEEP YOUR DRAGON

Before you grow a dragon, make sure
you have somewhere warm and cosy
for it to sleep. Hats are fine, but a
shoebox is ideal. They're big enough to
give your newly hatched dragon some
wriggle room, and you can tuck it under
your bed to keep your dragon safe and
out of sight.

Line your shoebox with something
soft and warm (something you don't
mind getting a few scorch marks!)

A jar lid makes an excellent
water tray.

Yoghurt pots are ideal for keeping

tasty dragon treats in. Keeping them well supplied should stop them wandering off to look for late-night snacks.

Decorating your shoebox will really make your dragon feel welcome and at home. Most dragons I've met seem to love glitter, and the shinier the better when it comes to sequins and gems.

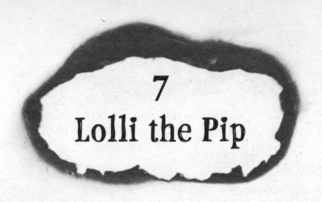

7
Lolli the Pip

Mum and Dad had called to ask if we could stay the night with Nana and Grandad – apparently Itsy and Bitsy had gone 'sightseeing' and the process of tracking down the two tarantulas had left half the contents of the house out in the garden and the other half in 'rather a muddle'. We didn't mind one bit. And to add to our delight, Nana had made a delicious apple pie for pudding, along with a huge jug of creamy custard, which unlike Mum's custard you didn't have to chew.

While Grandad cleared up and Nana settled down to do her crossword, I took Lolli upstairs to the room we shared whenever we stayed. She immediately bounced onto her bed by the window and burrowed under the covers to find her pyjamas, leaving her furry hat nestled by her pillow like a contented cat.

'Storeeeeee,' she demanded once she'd wriggled into them. She motioned to the notebook I'd pulled out of my bag.

'It's not a storybook, Lolli,' I said. 'It's a guide that I'm writing. A guide to growing dragons.'

Her eyes lit up and she did an extra big bounce off the bed and hurried over.

I flicked through the pages to show her what I'd written already.

'We'll have all the things we know about dragons in one ultimate guide,' I said.

'I wanna do it,' she said, starting to jiggle. 'I can draw and do lots of words. Big ones,' she added, giving me her best serious stare.

I thought about the amount of glue and glitter Lolli always used for her pictures and instinctively pulled the notebook back as her hand shot out to grab it.

'I'll get you some paper tomorrow, OK? I need it now to do my bit. Anyway it's your bedtime.'

She frowned and flumped back onto the bed.

I heard the creak of the stairs and Nana and Grandad came in to tuck her in.

'What's the trouble with Lolli?' Nana said as she burrowed further under the pillows, leaving only her spotty pyjama bottom showing.

'Not fair,' she mumbled. 'I wanna be big. Don't wanna go to bed.'

'Well, I'm going to bed in a minute and I'm not small,' Nana said with a chuckle. 'Come out so I can plant a kiss and let it grow into some lovely dreams.'

Lolli wriggled out enough for Nana to give her a kiss and for Grandad to tuck her back in.

'Nothing wrong with being small,' he said. 'Just think of the apples in that pie. All those pips Nana found inside them. They are as teeny-tiny as can be. But they each have a whole big apple tree waiting inside them. It's just a matter of time before they grow. But it's best not to rush these things. Now let's have some more of that story Nana's been reading us.'

Lolli yawned and reached for the knitted owl that Nana had made her. Almost before the first page was finished Lolli was fast asleep. Grandad picked up her scattered clothes while Nana put the book away and they both planted kisses on me too before heading back downstairs.

After they'd left I stared at my notebook, wondering what should come next in the guide.

'What do you think, Zing?'

Zing, who was clinging to my back, zapped away and for a second I wondered if he'd gone out into the garden. But then I heard a scratching from under the bed. I peered underneath and saw him in between two boxes. I grinned.

'Great idea!'

I pulled out the first box and rummaged through it until I'd found the envelope of photos we'd found that Elvi had buried under Grandad's shed. I smiled again when I saw the one of Elvi standing in the garden covered in dragons. I flicked through the ones of her and Arturo in Mexico, exploring the forest and finally discovering *La Ciudad Oculta de los Dragones*, the Hidden Dragon City.

THE STORY OF ELVI AND ARTURO

When people have travelled as much and seen as much as Elvi and Arturo, it's not easy to give a brief history of their lives. They really need a whole guidebook to themselves. But I've drawn some of the important bits for you. Elvi grew up in Iceland and Arturo in Mexico and they met as students. And that meeting changed their lives — and ours — forever!

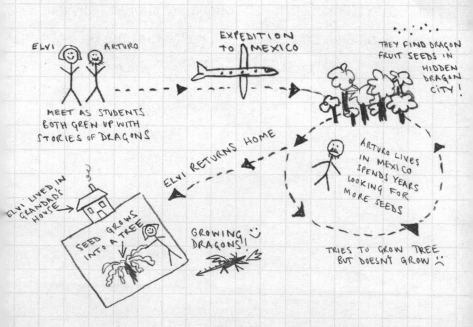

ELVI ARTURO

MEET AS STUDENTS
BOTH GREW UP WITH
STORIES OF DRAGONS

EXPEDITION
TO MEXICO

THEY FIND DRAGON
FRUIT SEEDS IN
HIDDEN
DRAGON
CITY!

ELVI RETURNS HOME

ARTURO LIVES
IN MEXICO
SPENDS YEARS
LOOKING FOR
MORE SEEDS

ELVI LIVED IN
GRANDAD'S
HOUSE →

SEED GROWS
INTO A TREE

GROWING
DRAGONS!!

TRIES TO GROW TREE
BUT DOESN'T GROW

I pulled out the map. I remembered Flicker's fiery breath lighting it up and revealing the Hidden Dragon City for the first time, and how excited I'd felt to see it. I held it up to the light, but that was no good; it needed dragon fire. I glanced over at Zing, who'd flown up onto the bed, but he didn't breathe flames so he couldn't help. Gazing out of the window I wished that Flicker would appear. Although given how big he was now, I wasn't sure I fancied holding up a flimsy piece of paper in front of one of his fiery breaths!

After looking through some more photos, I put the notebook under my pillow and pulled the quilt up over me. I closed my eyes, ready to dream of dragons.

8
Fizzling Fireworks and Flying Flickers

Instead of dreaming of dragons I woke up later with one in my face! Zing was flapping wildly right in front of me and I quickly rolled away before I got scratched by his claws. A bright burst of colour suddenly exploded outside the window, along with a thunderous bang that rattled the panes and startled Lolli awake. In a second she'd grabbed Owl, jumped out of her bed and leaped into mine.

I could feel her heart hammering as she clung to me.

'It's OK, Lollibob,' I said. 'It's just fireworks, I think.'

She peered out and said crossly, 'Too noisy.'

Then another bright burst of red lit up the window. But this time there was no bang and Lolli squealed with delight.

'Flicker!'

She scrambled over onto her own bed to peer out through the glass.

I joined her and pushed open the window to see Flicker's snout and sparkling diamond eyes properly. Above him another firework fizzled in the sky, though thankfully this one wasn't so loud.

'I won't be long,' I said to Lolli as Flicker moved closer.

'Can I come?' she said quietly.

'I'm sorry, Lolli,' I said. I just managed to stop myself from saying, 'You're too small.' I'd spent my life being the smallest one of my friends, and even though I was starting to sprout up now, just as Grandad had said I would, I remembered what it felt like to want to be bigger.

Lolli's bottom lip stuck out and she sniffed into Owl's head. I had a feeling he was about to get soggy.

'I need you to keep Zing company,' I said quickly.

'Doesn't he wanna come?'

'I don't think Zing likes fireworks very much,' I replied.

Zing flew down and landed on the bed. Little flashes of silver shot up and down his body, like he was shivering in colour. He hopped onto her lap and stretched his wings out across her legs. She let go of Owl with one hand and tapped him gently on the head.

'I'm good at looking after,' Lolli said.

'You're the best looker-afterer I know,' I replied.

I got onto the windowsill and then carefully
climbed onto Flicker. I heard a fierce yowl and spotted
a flash of ginger below us as Tomtom darted across the
garden and flung himself through the cat flap. He was
another one who hated fireworks. Once I was settled, I
turned back to give Lolli a wave. A second later Flicker
soared up into the sky and I glanced down at Grandad's
garden, lit up by strings of little solar lights hung along
the branches of the apple trees. Whoever owned the
field at the bottom of the garden was obviously having

a party and I saw a big white tent and a crowd of people staring up at the fireworks. I just hoped none of them would turn round and look in our direction!

But then I noticed the puffs of smoky cloud around us and knew that Flicker was well used to creating his own smoke-screen. I didn't need fireworks either, not with the sparks Flicker was blowing out, lighting up the sky. So I was glad when he flew away from the partygoers and the thumping music and the noisy bangs of the rockets.

Soon it was just us and a night sky filled with stars. I felt like I could almost reach up and pick them like apples from a tree. I remembered the first time I had ever ridden on Flicker's back and how tightly I'd clung on and lurched whenever he dipped and dived. Now though, the movements he made were so familiar that I didn't even have to think about it. Ted had said the same of riding on Sunny. We knew them so well and they knew us.

As we flew, I told Flicker all about the guide.

'There's a lot it would have been useful to know,' I said.

His scales rippled and a flash of colour moved up his body as he let out a gentle rumble.

I gripped tight as he suddenly shot upwards and curved back into a stomach-churning loop-the-loop.

FLYING TIPS

Trust your dragon. They're taking you for the ride of your life so don't expect to be in control. Or be able to steer. BUT if you spot danger you can help nudge them in the right direction by stroking the side of their neck you want them to turn towards. As their head instinctively turns, so will they.

Wear goggles. This helps stop the wind stinging your eyes and making them water. Swimming ones are fine, or even – if you're Ted – a scuba mask! I mean you're not in danger of looking uncool as no one except other dragon fliers is going to see you up there.

Grip tight with your knees, and if you're cold, hug your dragon – their scales will soon warm you up.

Don't forget your coat. Clouds are wet! Dragon scales will dry you off but it's not instant like waving a magic wand.

Best not to look down on your first few flights. You might think you have a head for heights but, believe me, going from ground level to cloud level in ten seconds is enough to shake the most seasoned rollercoaster rider.

Take a torch. If you're flying with friends, it's good to be able to signal to each other.

Take some snacks. You can never really tell how long you'll be up in the air and you can't exactly refuel on the way by dropping into your local corner shop for a bag of crisps. If dogs aren't allowed, I'm guessing dragons wouldn't be welcome! But beware — if you have a dragon who likes to loop the loop, don't eat before — or while — you fly!

9
Bee Careful . . .
Too Late!

When I clambered back into the room after our firework-lit flight, I found Zing still with Lolli, his wings now stretched over her tummy. He opened an eye, the bright sapphire blue one, but didn't move. I heard Lolli give a little murmur and saw her mouth pouting in her sleep and noticed a little shine on her cheeks and a sogginess to one side of Owl's head. Zing let out a gentle exhale that ruffled Lolli's hair and the pout disappeared.

'You're a good looker-afterer too,' I whispered to Zing.

I curled up in bed, wondering if Lolli was dreaming of flying.

I woke up to find Lolli cradling her flappy hat just like it was a cat. But then I noticed a flash of purple and orange and quickly realised it wasn't the hat that she was focusing on. Lolli still had the tiny bee dragon!

'Lolli,' I said, jumping out of bed and hurrying towards her. 'Don't stare at –'

But the 'it' didn't even bother leaping out of my mouth because I already knew it was too late. Lolli didn't turn around – her gaze was too fixed on the bee dragon nestled in the hat's fur. Any imprinting had happened long before I'd woken up.

IMPRINTING

Some birds fix their attention on the first creature they see when they hatch. They follow it to learn what they need to do. This is called imprinting. And dragons sometimes do this too.

Some birds, like goslings, imprint so strongly they don't even know they are a goose. If they imprint on a human, they'll think they are human too.

Luckily dragons know they are dragons. Which is probably just as well. Imagine a dragon trying to join you for Sunday dinner!

Dragons need a connection to fully imprint. It only happens when someone gazes into a dragon's eyes just after it emerges from its fruit and it holds that gaze. That's when the magic happens.

But be warned — if a dragon does imprint on you, it's your responsibility to keep that dragon safe.

'He's poorly,' Lolli whispered. 'What if I squidged him in the night?' she asked sadly.

'I'm sure you didn't,' I replied. 'I thought it was a bit strange that he didn't fly off when you were dancing around yesterday. I think he must have hurt himself and landed on your hat because it looked cosy and safe.'

Lolli's face brightened a little and she reached out a finger and let the brightly coloured bee dragon investigate the blob of jam on it.

'Careful,' I said. 'He might sting you.'

But Lolli shook her head. 'Pea's having seconds,' she said. 'He doesn't sting me. See?' And she giggled as the dragon stuck out a long yellow tongue and started licking up the jam.

'Pea?'

Lolli grinned and nodded. 'He's sweet. Sweet pea.'

Nana loved the sweet peas that Grandad had planted outside the kitchen window. Their colourful petals in shades of purple, pink and white almost looked like wings fluttering in the breeze. I had to admit it was the perfect name for this little dragon.

I peered down and inspected the dragon's wings. There didn't seem to be any damage. After Lolli's dragon Tinkle had hurt her wing, we'd learned that sometimes you just had to wait for things to heal. Hopefully jam and a bit of Lolli's looking after and this little dragon would be 'right as rain' again, as Grandad liked to say.

'Come on,' I said, 'let's take him out into the garden. Maybe he's fine and will just fly off if he sees another dragon to follow.'

Lolli carefully placed the furry hat on her head. 'Can he see?' she asked, her eyes straining upwards to try to catch a glimpse of the little dragon. I gave her a thumbs up as the dragon peeped out over the fur.

HOW TO TELL IF YOUR DRAGON IS A BOY OR A GIRL

You can't very easily!

For a long time I kept assuming every dragon that hatched from the fruit was a boy, just because I'm a boy. But Liam made me realise I couldn't know that for sure.

The only way to really know is to listen to what your dragon tells you. They'll usually let you know with a quick flick of their tail if they don't like the name you give them or how you refer to them. It seemed pretty clear Pea was quite happy with his name.

We found Grandad whistling in the kitchen. As we headed to the door he gave a long 'Whoaaa,' and then said, 'Hold your horses, you two. Nana's popped out and I'm on breakfast duties. No one's leaving this kitchen without a hearty breakfast. Jim's got himself some chickens and has just dropped off a batch of free-range delights, so who's for eggy bread?' He flipped a golden slice of toast in the sizzling frying pan and Lolli's hand shot up.

'He's been bending my ear about the chicken coop he's made,' Grandad said as he cooked. 'It's even got an upstairs, if you can believe it. He'll be making curtains next! But he's convinced there's a fox after his hens. They've been scared off laying this morning, and he said his lettuces have been shredded to bits and something's had a right go at his onions.'

We looked at each other, both clearly thinking the same thing.

There were definitely times when the dragons who

stayed for something to eat got a little too interested in the immaculate vegetable plot next door.

'I've been down to have a look myself this morning, and he's right about the mess, whole beds have been torn up,' Grandad went on, scratching his whiskery cheek. 'It's a lot more than we usually get from our little visitors, even the excitable ones.'

'You don't think it's actually a fox, do you?' I asked.

Grandad shrugged. 'Could well be. I reckon those hens will have caught their eye, that's for sure. I thought the holes that had popped up recently in the orchard were molehills, but I guess it could be foxes digging holes to bury what they catch. I've also noticed a bit of a stink round by the shed. And foxes are pretty whiffy.'

The piece of eggy bread I'd been chewing lodged stickily in my throat. I knew dragons had wings to fly out of the path of a fox, but newly hatched dragons often took a while to get airborne, as they cleaned off the gloopy mess of seeds and dragon-fruit skin.

What if not just Jim's hens but the glittery dragons had caught the eye of a hungry fox? Foxes were fast and clever. A tiny dragon would stand no chance against an attack from such an expert hunter.

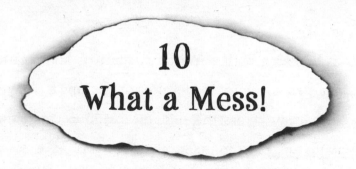

10
What a Mess!

I stuffed the last of the eggy bread into my mouth and, mumbling my thanks to Grandad, dashed outside. I kept picturing the glint in a fox's eye as it slyly stalked a tiny dragon. It sent a shiver like a startled snake slithering down my back. I skidded to a halt past the apple trees, taking in the mess, and then started scanning the ground. Picking my way through the rows of vegetables, I hardly dared to look in case I found something; and then when I didn't, I just felt the snake slithering down further as I wondered what that meant too. Would the little dragons be a bite-sized snack, leaving nothing behind?

Zing darted about above me as usual and didn't

seem bothered by the mushy cucumbers and splatted raspberries, the uprooted lettuces or the tangle of sweet peas that lay across the dirt, the bamboo canes they grew up tugged from the ground.

I checked the dragon-fruit tree, which thankfully looked unscathed. There was only a handful of ripe fruits left, the rest having burst during the night. I just hoped their dragons had flown straight off and not lingered in the garden. Messy pulp and scraps of dragon-fruit skin littered the ground, and in one place it looked as if it had been smeared across the soil. I shuddered as an image barged into my mind of a fox dragging an

unsuspecting baby dragon away before it had even stretched its wings.

I kicked myself for not staying longer so I could be there to protect them. I thought about setting up Grandad's tent, but the idea of camping on my own without the superhero squad made me feel a bit jumpy. And besides I could still see some very green fruit on the tree. There was no way I could keep watch all night, every night until they were ripe. I needed a plan to keep them safe whether I was there or not.

But what plan? Jim's chicken coop looked like a fortress and the fox was still undeterred. I wondered if

Jim would be setting traps next. I pictured a fox caught and frightened and suddenly remembered Grandad saying foxes were only trying to look after their families. I'd been picturing the fox as some kind of evil baddie, but now my mind was filled with the faces of a handful of hungry little cubs waiting expectantly back in their den. I hoped Jim wouldn't go as far as traps. No, there had to be another way of keeping the dragons safe. And best to do it soon, just in case Jim did take matters into his own hands.

Lolli joined me by the tree, cradling her fur hat and stroking Pea's upturned head. A flickering tongue shot out of his long snout and licked her finger.

'I don't think he can fly,' she said sadly.

I was about to try to reassure her when there was a crash behind us.

One of the flowerpots perched on the shed windowsill lay smashed on the ground. Zing, who was flapping soil from his wings and looking dazed, flew over to me.

He landed on my arm and I brushed the rest of the dirt off his head. Frankly, it was enough work making sure Zing didn't get into trouble, and now there was a poorly bee dragon and a flurry of new dragons that might be about to face a fox. When Flicker had first burst from his fruit and flapped into my life, I'd had to protect him from Tomtom, my tiger-hearted cat. Now I needed to add 'protect from foxes' to the list too.

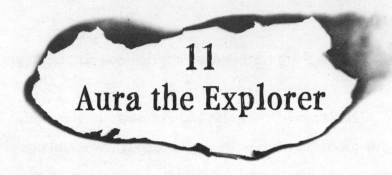

11
Aura the Explorer

Later, at home, I started searching online for ways to deter foxes. I'd just scribbled down 'flashing lights' when a message popped up from Aura.

> **Aura**
> Hola!
> How's the guide going? I bet you've already written loads! I'm seeing Arturo again this afternoon. Every time we meet up and he catches sight of Rosebud his eyes shine like dragon fire! I wish you'd been there to see his face when I handed him the seedling I brought for him from our tree! He's spent

his WHOLE life hoping to grow dragons and now he actually can!

He's shown me loads of photographs of him and my amma on their expeditions into the rainforest. Can you imagine how they felt finding the Hidden Dragon City? It must have been AMAZING!! I'm going to be an explorer just like them!

He's TOTALLY 100% SURE that there was a third seed in that temple they found. Obviously we know that there were two seeds resting on the claws of the golden dragon foot. But the foot had three claws and he's convinced there was another seed there once, one for each claw. And the missing seed was dislodged – or taken. When Elvi's seed grew and his didn't, he began a quest to find the third seed. An actual quest!

First he searched the temple, then he combed the area in case an animal had scattered it. He did that for years and years and years, getting deeper and deeper into the forest, recording every inch of the land in minute detail. But although he found heaps of other things, like new insects and plants, there was never any sign of the seed. Of course, it could have just been eaten and destroyed, but he doesn't believe that for a second. And neither do I!

While he's been on his quest he's heard stories from people he's met, telling of flickering lights in the sky over the forest and glimpses of strange horned birds. He believes these were actually dragons, and that the seed was taken from the city and planted – or maybe simply dropped – somewhere in the depths of the forest. I just wish we could help him find it.

Now tell me everything that is happening with you!

Aura

PS Rosebud is loving it here! And Mamma's dragon has found us too!!

I'm so glad Mamma can see her again. She remembers all the games they used to play together, and I'm starting to think that Mamma liked to play tricks on Amma. She would never let me get away with half the things she's telling me she did! Mamma's dragon's name is Dreki, which is 'dragon' in Icelandic. Isn't that wonderful?

DREKI

Type:
Hypno-dragon

Physical characteristics:
Rose-pink, slender,
four pink wings like a
dragonfly's, ruby eyes.
Breath a ripple of colour
like a rainbow.

Diet: Most plants and fruit
but particularly
loves rhubarb.

Special skills: Wings pulse
different colours and can hypnotise.

Dragonality: Shy, strong, clever.

Warning: Don't look directly at her wings unless
you want to forget you've seen a dragon. Aura's
poor mum once startled her so much she was
hypnotised. And she might never have seen
dragons again if it hadn't been for Grandad
helping her to remember.

I leaned back in my chair and let my eyes run back over her words. We already knew from the letters we'd found that Arturo had been looking for a third seed. I'd been amazed at how determined he was, how he kept looking even after years of never finding anything. But then I thought of how desperate I'd been when the dragon-fruit seedlings I'd been looking after had started dying. And I knew I'd have done the exact same thing. I'd have kept going for the sake of the dragons.

But could he really be so sure that the seed was out there to be found? Clearly Aura believed it was, and she was all set to leap into his footsteps to find it herself. Aura the explorer. I pictured her setting off into the rainforest. Then I looked out of the window onto our little garden below, with its tatty lawn and straggly borders. There wasn't much to explore on my doorstep. Even Grandad's garden was tamer these days! Suddenly, in comparison to quests and hiking into rainforests, nothing I had to say sounded very exciting. And being distracted by foxes meant I hadn't even done as much of the guide as I'd have liked.

I started writing a new message and found myself addressing it to Ted instead.

Tomas

Hi, Ted,

What do you know about foxes? Also, do you fancy doing some fact files on our dragons? I've done them for Flicker and Zing and Dreki, Aura's mum's dragon, but I could do with some help.

Thanks.

By the time I'd grabbed a drink and a snack, a message had pinged back.

Ted

Sorry, Tomas, we're heading out for dinner in a minute. The food here is amazing. Dad's signed me

---

up for a cooking course at the weekend. I can't wait.

So for now it'll have to be what I know about foxes off the top of my head:

They're a member of the dog family, but they can retract their claws like a cat and have vertical pupils like a cat. And grey foxes can climb trees. You won't find dogs doing that!

They use the whiskers on their face and legs to help navigate and even use the earth's magnetic field to hunt. How cool is that!

A group of foxes is called a 'skulk' or 'leash'. A male is a 'dog fox' or something else which I can't remember. Females are 'vixen'. Young foxes are kits or cubs or pups.

They live in underground dens and the dog fox hunts and brings food back to the kits.

They secrete a VERY smelly smell from their scent glands. And their poo is super-stinky. Do you remember when Dexter rolled in it? Kat and Kai had to give him about six baths with tomato ketchup as shampoo before they got rid of the smell!

Foxes are very caring. I read about this one cub who got caught in a snare and it stayed alive because its mother brought it food till it was rescued.

I'm definitely up for doing some fact files. Leave it with me!

And let me know if you need me to look into foxes more. I'm sure I can find out loads.

I grinned. All that off the top of his head! I knew fact-tastic Ted would be the person to ask. Now I just had to see if there was anything in that list that might help me figure out how to divert a fox away from some plump hens and a crop of new dragons. It was a relief to have some help on the dragon profiles too. Fact files were right up Ted's street, and one less thing for me to worry about.

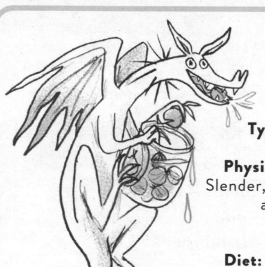

SUNNY

Type: Fire dragon

Physical characteristics: Slender, golden yellow scales, a frill of spines round neck.

Diet: Anything! (So be warned!) But particularly likes pickled onions, banana pancakes, marrows and s'mores.

Special skills: Fire power, speed, strength and agility. Also marshmallow toasting for the best s'mores ever – if you're careful.

Dragonality: Adaptable (especially when it comes to food), resourceful (especially when it comes to food), adventurous (especially when it comes to food), very caring.

Warning: highly explosive digestive habits, so monitor feeding time closely. If you see his belly pulsing with a fiery orange glow like flames are sizzling through him, take cover!

TED AND SUNNY'S
CHOCOLATE S'MOREANATOR

- 2 chocolate biscuits
- 1 big marshmallow
- 1 chunk of chocolate
- Chocolate sauce
- Chocolate sprinkles

— Ask your friendly dragon to toast the marshmallow.

— Put your toasted marshmallow onto your first biscuit and squidge the chunk of chocolate into your melty marshmallow.

— Then add the second chocolate biscuit and press down.

— Drizzle with chocolate sauce and sprinkle with sprinkles!

— Eat in private — it's messy!

12
Mud Pools to Mountains

When I crawled into bed that night, I hoped that Dad was right about your brain sorting out problems while you got on with something else, like sleeping. He always says that if you're banging your head against something, bake a cake or go for a walk or just sleep on it. And then once you're scoffing the cake or you wake up in the morning, the answer will be right there twiddling its thumbs, or possibly licking its fingers, and rolling its eyes as if it's been there all along.

I hoped he was right, because all I'd come up with so far was . . . well, nothing.

But I didn't dream of cunning ways to distract a fox, I dreamed of flying. I was gliding over lava fields, gazing out across wings that beat slow and steady. I saw vast stretches of blackened land that looked swollen and cracked like scales, followed by jagged rocks that stuck up like spines along a great dragon's back.

This was the land where Flicker lived. The Land of the Far North. Where dragons erupted from volcanoes in glorious technicolour and filled the air with song.

Each time I dreamed of this place, I saw it in more detail. Red and purple mud pools that bubbled and steamed, sprawling lakes with islands rising from crystal blue waters and patches of white ice swirling across the rock along their shores. And tonight a great cavernous crater filled with a green pool, like a giant dragon eye staring up at the stars.

When I woke my heart was still racing over the skies and it took a minute to slow it down. As I wiped the sleep from my eyes, I couldn't help noticing that no great ideas were perched on my bed waiting for me. And the feeling of soaring immediately turned into a stomach-churning nosedive.

Which is exactly what Zing seemed to do as he zoomed down from the shelf above my desk and landed in a tumbling heap on the quilt in front of me. His oversized wings still sometimes got the better of him, and I gently lifted him up to save him the embarrassment of a mad wriggle to get right side up.

'You looked like you needed a bit of help there,' I said as the air crackled around him.

He nudged my hand with his snout and looked at me, his sapphire eye as blue as the crystal water I'd flown over. He twisted his head and I saw the swirling cloud of his other eye light up with a flash, like a lightning bolt shooting across it. My hand buzzed with

the energy and magic of the little dragon in front of me.

'You're right,' I said. 'You're not the only one who needs a bit of help.'

Luckily, I had the whole superhero squad at my fingertips, and Kat and Kai were expert planners. They were bound to have a Plan with a capital P.

First thing in the morning was a good time to catch up with the twins in China, so a couple of minutes later the screen was full of their smiling faces.

'*Zaoan!*' they chorused, as I waved and then expertly lunged across my desk to stop Zing sending a glass of water flying with his tail.

'I know you miss us, but I'm not sure you can actually dive through the computer to get to us,' Kat said.

'Got your hands full?' Kai asked, as Zing flew up onto my shoulder and I set the glass down.

'Just a bit,' I replied.

I quickly explained about the possible fox attack in Grandad's garden and sent them Ted's off-the-top-of-his-head fox fact file.

'I read that they don't like flashing lights, but unless I'm going to stand there blinking a torch on and off, I'm not sure what to do about that,' I said sadly.

Kai scanned Ted's info and looked thoughtful. 'It sounds as if this fox is probably just after food for his cubs, so maybe you should make it really easy for him. If you put out a load of tasty snacks, I bet he wouldn't bother hassling the hens or the dragons. I mean, our dad would choose take-out over hunting for tea any day.'

'That's a great idea! So what do foxes like to eat?' I asked.

Kai shrugged and Kat pulled a don't-look-at-me face.

'Don't worry, I can find out,' I said. 'So how about you? You must have your hands full too.'

I still couldn't believe they'd found another active

dragon-fruit tree. We'd always thought ours was the only one left. But it was definitely a relief to know that not only was there another one, but there could be even more out there, waiting to be found.

'Not really,' Kat said. 'There was only one fruit left when we found the tree, and the dragon didn't hang around for long.'

'We're keeping a close eye on it though,' Kai added hurriedly. 'There's already more fruit starting to grow so there should be another crop soon.'

'I'm glad you're keeping watch,' I said.

'We're not the only ones,' muttered Kat.

'What do you mean?'

'Oh, nothing,' Kai jumped in. 'Ignore her. She said she had this feeling we were being watched while we were watching the tree. But I didn't see anything.'

'Just because you didn't see, doesn't mean no one was there.' Kat scowled and elbowed Kai in the side.

I sensed the twins were about to lock horns.

'So how are Crystal and Dodger?' I asked, hoping talking about their dragons would stop the quarrel.

They both turned in unison and their eyes lit up.

'They've been taking us aerial sightseeing!' declared Kai. 'We've seen so many beautiful gardens and pagodas.'

'And there are all these zigzagging bridges in Suzhou so they keep slaloming back and forth in line with them,' Kat added, laughing.

'And last night,' Kai went on, 'they took us over Tianping Shan – Flat Heaven Mountain – and around Taihu! It's this ancient lake and it's huge and has loads of little islands, and during the day they're keeping out of sight on one of them, just like they do at the nature reserve near you.'

CRYSTAL

Type: Ice dragon

Physical characteristics:
Purple and electric blue,
spikes like icicles under
jaw. Wings have
swirling patterns.

Diet: Insects mostly, but
likes frozen peas as a treat.

Special skills: Creates ice blasts
and snow, makes the best ice
sculptures and frost art,
expert slushy maker.

Dragonality: Creative, sociable, quite
competitive, cooperative (although not
always with Dodger).

Warning: Crystal is generally friendly,
both with people and dragons, but can
lock horns with Dodger. Watch out
for her icy blast!

DODGER

Type: Sneaker dragon

Physical characteristics:
Vivid greeny-blue scales.
Peacock-feather design
on wings with yellow-
and-blue eye shapes
leading to outer edge.

Diet: Quite fussy and very
often changes his mind about
what he likes and dislikes.

Special skills: Camouflage to the point
of invisibility.

Dragonality: Playful, energetic, a bit of a
prankster.

Warning: Excellent at sneak attacks and
enjoys making people jump!

13
Attack of the Flying Strawberry

Grandad's garden looked in a bigger mess than ever when I arrived. I could see Jim over the fence busy cooing to his hens and holding up some flowery material. It looked like he actually was planning on making them curtains! But at least that was better than making traps.

'Foxes are omnivores,' Grandad had said when I'd started rummaging in their kitchen cupboard. 'Which means they're happy eating berries and fruit as well as the mice and rabbits they hunt. They'll also help themselves to whatever they can find, including what's in the bins.'

'Not very fussy then,' I'd replied, eyeing the bin and

trying to decide if I wanted to go fishing about in there.

'Not very, no. We just need to not leave too much food out because it might attract rats. I don't think Nana'll thank us if we start serving up picnics for them!'

Standing by the dragon-fruit tree, I scoured the hedges at the bottom of the garden that bordered the field and wondered where would be the best place to leave the food we'd gathered. If the fox came across it as soon as it set foot in the garden, it would hopefully leave Jim's hens and any dragons well alone.

I found the perfect spot and laid out strawberries, redcurrants and a mushy ripe banana. And then I reached into my bag to get the tin of dog food I'd taken from Mum's emergency pet-food supply. It certainly smelled strong enough to catch the attention of a hungry fox. I was just peering back into the hedge when I heard Grandad give a cry.

'What are you playing at, you daft apeth?'

I hurried over and found him staring up at the shed roof.

'Crikey, you were right about that smell,' I said, wafting a hand in front of my face. 'Foxes definitely have a way of letting you know they've been visiting.'

'I'm less bothered about the smell right now than this earwig rain we're having,' Grandad said.

He brushed his hair and a load of earwigs tumbled into his open hand.

'Zing's swish-swashing tail has been covering me with moss and crawlies,' he said. 'I don't know what's got into him, but he won't come down from up there.'

I called Zing's name, but he didn't even turn around. All I could see was the tip of his lightning-bolt tail flicking from side to side over the edge of the roof.

'I'd better see what the trouble is,' I said, and climbed up onto the bench.

As my head reached the level of Zing's tail, he suddenly stretched out his wings and I saw flashes of silver shoot across them. I peered round him, wondering what had got him so alarmed, and got a face full of mushy strawberry, which startled me so much I nearly toppled backwards off the bench. I quickly wiped it away, keeping my eyes fixed on the flash of orange that was hopping feverishly from clawed foot to clawed foot on the other side of the shed roof. And then I ducked as another sweet-smelling missile soared past me.

Although I appreciated Zing's attempt to shield me, I decided I needed to get a better look at this dragon, so I shuffled further along the bench. It watched us, its horned head twisting quickly back and forth as it tried to keep us both in its sights. It had a collar of spikes and

more spines running down its back and it had not one but two bright orange tails. They each ended in a pincer, and it was these that it was using to fling missiles at us.

I raised a hand, hoping it might sense that I meant it no harm. But it immediately arched its long slender body like a cat about to hiss. And then it pounded the roof with each tail in a rhythmic thumping war cry. It opened its mouth and I quickly grabbed hold of Zing and leaped down. A second later a crackling blast of golden fire erupted from the roof.

'I think it might be time to take cover,' Grandad said, and we dashed into the shed and pushed the door shut.

'They're not usually that feisty or fiery,' he declared.

'Or unfriendly,' I added. 'I mean, I know we've had the odd startled dragon let out a warning belch or something, but that one was aiming straight for my head!'

There was more thumping from the roof, and then a skittering of claws and we peered out the window in time to see the dragon leap onto the branch of the tree and disappear into the leaves.

'Looks like you've got more than foxes to worry about, hey, Chipstick?' Grandad said.

I nodded.

You know, sometimes growing vegetables had its appeal. You wouldn't catch a cucumber trying to fry your hair.

CUCUMBERS V DRAGONS:
THINGS CUCUMBERS DO NOT DO

Scorch so many holes in your pants they look like you could use them as a sieve. Though who in their right mind would use pants as a sieve I don't know.

Shred your homework to line a shoebox nest (as an excuse it's definitely better than 'my dog ate it' but it still doesn't work, so I wouldn't bother trying).

Use next door's washing line for some fiery target practice.

Fly at your face. Especially when your face is not expecting it.

Unleash poos that explode — or any kind of poos for that matter. Vegetables are

121

very easy to clean up after. Oh yes, in case you don't already know, dragon poo has a nasty habit of exploding when it dries out. So get ready for:

POO PATROL!

Here's what you'll need:

- Water pistol: to keep the dragon poo wet and stop it exploding!
- Oven gloves: to pat out any stray sparks.
- Spade: to scoop up and throw the poo down the toilet. Just remember to flush!

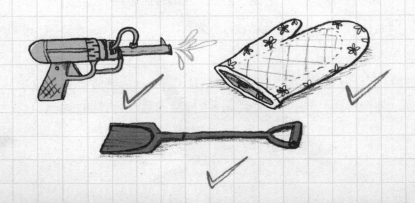

14
Batman and Moose and Bee Makes Three

Since Nana and Grandad were heading out for the afternoon, they dropped me home in time for lunch.

'Maybe give that fiery fella a chance to fly off,' Grandad said. 'Not sure I like the idea of you facing that one without me there to lend a hand.'

At home, I grabbed the sandwiches Dad had made for me and hurried upstairs before any holiday chores could be flung my way. I had quite enough on my plate.

While I ate, Zing started scrabbling across my floor, dragging his oversized wings and scratching at the carpet with his tail. Little flecks of silver shot across his body. This was Zing's idea of a light lunch, charging

up with static from the carpet. Still, it meant he wasn't draining the batteries in my remote-control helicopter – for the gazillionth time. I stuffed the last mouthful in as Zing flared brightly and zapped out of sight. I scanned the room, wondering where he'd pop up, and braced myself in case it turned out to be right in front of my face. But there was no sign of him and instead what popped up was a message from Liam.

> **Liam**
> I'm sooooooooooo bored. Send help.

I didn't like to tell Liam that right now boring sounded

quite good to me, what with Zing's zapping and wily foxes and fiery-breathed, pincer-flinging dragons. And a bee dragon who still wasn't going anywhere.

I thought about Liam's dragon, Maxi.

He'd been pretty hard to handle when he'd first burst out of the fruit, way back before Liam was a member of the superhero squad. I remembered seeing him looking worse for wear on several occasions and thought back to the first time I'd seen Maxi, on our class trip. Maxi had got so alarmed his spikes stuck out like a puffer fish. And his green breath had started super-sizing everything in sight.

I quickly typed out a reply to Liam.

Tomas

Sending help, and then need you to send it straight back. Have got angry dragon on my hands. Any clever ideas?

Luckily, with no time difference Liam's reply pinged back only moments later.

Liam

You need armour! With Maxi I used my mum's old moped helmet and my skateboard pads in case I needed to dive or roll out the way. And a frying pan for a shield. Good luck and keep your eyes open. Remember, it could have sneak attack!

It wasn't totally reassuring. I only had my bike helmet, which didn't cover my face, and no skateboarding gear. I could probably find the shield, but was I really going to spend my whole time lugging that around?

MAXI

Type: Activator dragon

Physical characteristics:
Big, with grey scales and lime green ones underneath, neat row of spines down back, jagged spiked tail.

Diet: Vegetables, fruit.

Special skills: Can activate dragon fruits and dragon-fruit trees by breathing on them, so they will grow dragons!

Warning: Maxi's green breath also has super-sizing ability, which can make things grow super-big and super-fast! His breath has healing properties too. If alarmed, will puff up in defence like a puffer fish, with scales and spines sticking out to make himself bigger.
Very rare.

I'd have to hope the dragon would leave soon. But I had a nasty feeling that it was the same orange dragon that Grandad and I had seen flying into the shed window on Saturday. Which meant it had already hung around longer than the others. What was keeping it here?

There was a tap at my bedroom door and Lolli's head peered in.

'Tomas, come see,' she whispered.

I followed her into her bedroom, stepping over the stick hospital Lolli had officially opened some time ago and that was still taking up most of the floor.

'Careful,' she scolded as my foot landed dangerously close to a short stubby stick with a plaster binding its twiggy leg. The leg was actually sticking out at a pretty uncomfortable-looking right angle.

'Larisa is nearly all better,' she said proudly. 'She got medals for karate and ballet.'

Then she waved me closer and pointed to the fairy boot that sat on the little table by her window. One fairy was happily swinging in the little half-conker-shell swing seat and another was wedged sideways on the slide that formed the tongue of the boot. With the boot pulled open, I could see a Lego Batman inside in one of the rooms. He was standing on a petal-leaf chair, having tea with a small moose at the spotty toadstool table. But that obviously wasn't what she wanted me to see.

In one of the beds that swung like a hammock from the open side of the boot lay a very contented-looking bee dragon. Lolli had lined the bed with cotton wool and put a bottle top filled with jam on top.

'Er . . . very cosy,' I said.

Lolli beamed and then snatched up a piece of paper lying by her bed, sending glittery sparkles flying in every direction.

'I'm going to be a dragon vet,' she declared proudly. 'I know lots of things. See,' she added, laying the paper out on the table. 'But I don't know everything. So I have to go to big school for a really, really long time to get qualtified.'

I nodded and smiled as I read. At least with Lolli on the job, I didn't need to worry about the bee dragon. Although it was pretty clear she still had flying on her mind.

Lolli's Vet guide

Dragons with toof ake are grumpy.
They need cudalls.
Dragons with porly tummies are sad.
They need cudalls.
Dragons with sor throts are fed up.
They need iscreem and cudalls.
Dragons with herty wings are bored.
They need a big sparkerly plarster
and cudalls.
Porly dragons need stories and cudalls
and choclit.

Then she pulled out another piece of paper covered in shiny sticky gems, rainbow stickers and little gluey mountains of glitter.

'And,' she said importantly, 'I saw your Flicker fact file and I wroted my own.'

LOLLI'S FACT FILE

Tinkle likes singing and cudalls. She is small. She has silver bloo scals. She is the most best dragon of all. I love Tinkle.

15
Sir Laughalot Meets Arturo

I spent the rest of the afternoon trying to fashion some armour. I ended up wearing my bike helmet covered in tin foil (for extra heat-resistance) with a colander taped to it in front of my face. I'd also borrowed my Mum's quilted jacket and made a breastplate with the rest of the tape and two baking trays to hang over my shoulders. I figured that would

give me some padding and good fireproofing.

With a frying pan as a shield, I stood looking at myself in the tall mirror in my parents' room. I'm not going to lie – I wasn't exactly your shining Knight of the Round Table. Move over Sir Lancelot, make room for Sir Laughalot.

Of course, Aura chose that exact moment to video call. Mum came hurrying into the room and then skidded to a halt when she saw me.

'It's Aura,' she said, peering at my face through the colander holes as if she wasn't quite sure I was in there. 'Calling for a chat from Mexico.' She held up my phone in front of her face and grinned and waved at the screen.

I shook my head madly, jangling, trying to make her realise that I didn't want to be beamed across the world in my current state.

I started backing away before she could turn the phone around and point Aura in my direction, but just managed to trip over a pile of clothes and land in a clanging heap on the floor.

Mum stared down at me, puzzled. 'I think he's playing knights in armour,' she said to Aura. 'Hold on, he'll be with you in a sec.'

Scowling, I took the phone from her, muttering that it was nothing to do with playing or knights.

Aura hardly blinked when she saw me, which probably stopped my face exploding from the blazing redness that had spread across it.

Grateful, I hastily explained about the fiery orange dragon and the need for better protection, taking my armour off noisily as I did.

'Good luck, it sounds like you're going to need it,' she said when the last piece of armour had clanged to the ground. 'I think Kat needs some too. Did she tell you that she thinks someone's watching the dragon-fruit tree? And she's already counted twenty fruits growing!'

'I'm hoping she's wrong about being watched,' I said. 'But with that many fruits they're definitely going to have their hands full. So how about you?' I asked. 'What are you up to?'

Her face lit up. 'I'm going exploring, Tomas! I'm so excited!! Mama and Papi promised me an adventure and it's really happening! Can you believe it?' Her voice was almost tripping over itself in gleeful excitement.

'That sounds brilliant,' I said.

And then she panned the camera across the room and Arturo stepped into view.

'*Encantado de conocerte*, Tomas,' he said giving me a wave.

His face was so familiar from the photos I'd seen, but it was still a shock to see him standing right there.

'It's very good to meet you, Tomas,' he said in English,

smiling. 'The boy who grew dragons!'

I stared back at him, feelings rushing so fast through me I felt I might get swept away. I'd got to know Arturo through his letters. He and Elvi had taught me so much. But I never thought I'd get to speak to him. And it looked like I wouldn't now, because as the torrent of feelings rushed on, I opened my mouth but couldn't actually get any words out.

Luckily Aura jumped back in, which gave me a few seconds to pull myself together.

'We're going up the river in a boat because it would take too long hiking through the forest,' said Aura. 'But it'll still be a few days before we reach the Hidden City.'

'You're going to the Hidden City?' I asked, incredulous.

She nodded excitedly. 'We've got a satellite phone so I can still send you messages.' Reaching down, she picked something up and waved it at the screen. 'And look – I've got a proper explorer's journal too. I'm going to follow Amma's example and record everything!'

'Aura has told me how you found the map, Tomas.' Arturo said. 'And discovered its secrets,' he added, sounding impressed.

I nodded, buying myself another few seconds to unjumble the words tumbling into my mouth. 'It was Flicker who showed us. His breath lit up the map and revealed the city. We'd never have seen it without him.'

Arturo smiled. 'You have earned their trust. *Bien hecho*. You've done well, Tomas.'

At those words a sudden tingle of warmth spread all through me like I'd just leaned against dragon scales.

I wanted to tell him what his letters had meant to me, and how without him and Elvi we'd never have shared the magic of the dragons, but before I could, Zing zapped out of nowhere right in front of my face, making me reel back.

'So, this must be Zing,' Arturo said, laughing as the dragon flew up onto my shoulder and settled there.

Arturo's face leaned towards the screen, as if he didn't want to miss one tiny detail. I smiled and opened my palm so Zing could hop onto it, then lifted him closer to the camera.

Zing peered into the lens and Arturo's eyes shone bright as the two of them greeted each other with a bob of the head. Then Zing suddenly curled his tail up over his back and unleashed a tiny bolt of lightning that leaped between the tip of his zigzag tail and his horn. The arc of light writhed in the air, emitting a high-pitched buzzing sound, and as he moved his tail the zinging note changed as if he was playing an electrifying fanfare especially for Arturo. It was something I'd never seen him do before.

'*Extraordinario!*' cried Arturo, clapping his hands.

And Zing's flash of lightning turned from electric blue to white to vivid orange and back again. He certainly knew how to impress! And once again I wondered how much else there was to learn about my dragon.

'I have dreamed of dragons my whole life,' Arturo whispered, still mesmerised by Zing's display. 'But even my dreams did not prepare me for how wonderful they are. *Mágico. Mágico!*'

16
Sleeping Dragon, Racing Dragon

After talking to Arturo I was buzzing, and wished with every atom of my being that I was there with them, packing for an expedition to the Hidden City. I closed my eyes and pictured stepping onto the boat, the rainforest thrumming with life around me and the humid air making my sleeves stick to my arms. I was so caught up in my daydream that when the computer pinged my brain started inventing strange animals that might make pinging noises. When I finally emerged from my daydream, blinking at the bright glare of reality, I saw that a message had arrived from Kat.

I glanced at the clock on the computer. It was after midnight in China. I opened the message, hoping nothing was wrong. Aura's reminder about their fears of being watched was still fresh in my mind.

> **Kat**
>
> Hi Tomas,
>
> Are you there? Can you chat?

I quickly replied that I was and waited for the call to start. A few seconds later their grinning faces filled the screen and I breathed a sigh of relief that it obviously wasn't bad news they had to share.

'You're up late,' I said. 'Nothing's wrong, is there?'

'Not at all! We've just been out flying with Crystal and Dodger!' Kai said excitedly, and then got a shove from Kat and a warning glance at the door as she put her finger to her lips.

He carried on in more of a whisper. 'They took us

to the Yu Garden again. I'm sending you some photos of the dragon walls we told you about.'

The pictures popped up and I marvelled at them.

'I can't believe you're actually seeing all this in real life,' I said.

'Just wait till you hear about the Dragon Backbone Rice Terraces,' Kat said. 'I can't wait to see those. The name in Mandarin is *Longsheng titian* – it means the *earthen fields won by the dragon.*'

'Nainai told us we have to visit them while we're here,' Kai went on. 'We were hoping Crystal and Dodger could fly us to see them, but it turns out they're at Longsheng, which is a really long way away, so we're going to have to wait until the holidays to go. The terraces look just like the backbone of a dragon. How cool is that! Maybe it's actually a sleeping dragon and we'll wake it up!'

'We're seeing dragons everywhere here,' said Kat. 'It's brilliant!'

'It sounds amazing,' I said.

'Anyway, while we were flying we started thinking we should send something for the guide about dragons in China. They're really important in Chinese culture.'

'Yeah,' went on Kai. 'You know we were saying that dragons are usually the villains in stories? Well, here it's not like that at all. They're seen as kind and powerful and wise and they protect people. Just like our dragons!'

'We've also found out that Asian dragons really love water,' Kat said. 'They usually live near it or in it. The dragon-fruit tree we found is right by the river, so I think that's where the dragon we saw bursting out of its

fruit must have headed. It certainly didn't stay around for long.'

'So what do you think?' Kai asked. 'About putting this stuff in the guide?'

'I think it sounds like a brilliant idea,' I said.

The screen suddenly filled with a picture that Kai was holding up. I thought I could make out wings and maybe a tail, but I couldn't see it properly because he was holding it upside down and far too close to the camera. Kat pulled his hand back and turned the picture the right way round.

'I was hoping you'd say that!' he said. 'Here's a picture of one of the boats from the Duanwu Jie.'

'You know we told you about the dragon-boat festival we went to?' Kat added. 'There are these really cool wooden boats shaped and decorated like dragons that people paddle and race.'

'It's a massive festival,' Kai said. 'You'd love it. Maybe next year you could even come and visit.'

By the time I got to bed that night my head was brimming with bright, colourful images of Mexico, and thoughts of soaring over sleeping dragons in China, so that when I closed my eyes and started dreaming it felt like I was exploring those places too. Which is why I couldn't help feeling a bit disappointed to wake up in the morning and find myself in my room, with Dad waving a feather duster at me.

It looked like the furthest I'd be exploring was under the bed.

17
Sweet and Stinky

When I passed Lolli's bedroom on my way down to breakfast, I spotted her tucking all her stick patients back into bed. Seeing me, she picked the furry hat up from the table, gently placed it on her head and then skipped towards me. The tiny bee dragon peeped out over the fuzzy rim.

'It might be a bit hot for that hat today,' I said. 'It's boiling out there already.'

She shrugged. 'But Pea likes it. He can see better, and it's like flying. Where you going? I wanna come.'

I thought of the flames shooting off the top of the shed.

'Maybe you should keep Pea here,' I said. 'Just till I can make sure the orange dragon has left.'

'But we can help,' she said, looking up at me hopefully.

'Sorry, Lolli – I've only got enough armour for me.'

She frowned and then stomped back into her bedroom. She'd have probably slammed the door behind her, but sticky Larisa was leaning nonchalantly against it. If sticks could glare, I had a feeling Larisa would be eyeing me crossly.

I decided not to walk to Nana and Grandad's in full armour. It might only be a two minute and forty-five second walk to get there, but I'd have to pass the playground. The last thing I needed was some Year Seven kid spotting me. I had enough wriggly worms in my tummy about starting secondary school in the autumn without getting on the bus on the first day and being crowned 'Colander King'.

At their back door, I paused to suit up. I stood there

fiddling with the colander mask that kept slipping off and gently boiling under the tin-foil helmet which was quickly heating up in the sun. After a few minutes Nana and Grandad came out to sit on the bench in the shade and drink their morning cuppa.

'You're looking . . . shiny,' Nana said, sipping her tea. 'Robot?'

Grandad shook his head. 'This isn't dressing up for the fun of it – it looks to me like he's come prepared. You've got some great protection there, Chipstick!'

'Oh dear, are you having problems with the –'

here Nana paused, looked both ways then whispered – 'local residents.'

I nodded. Nana had hardly batted an eyelid when she'd found out there were dragons growing in her garden. It had, she declared, explained where all her jam tarts and fruit pies went. (Of course, actually that was Grandad squirrelling them away for us in his secret stash of goodies in the shed!) Nana always took great care not to mention 'the D-word' out loud though, in case anyone discovered our secret. She was as protective of the dragons as we were.

'It all looked quiet down there first thing,' Grandad said. 'No sign of our fiery visitor. Only Jim who spent a good half-hour bending my ear about his unhappy hens. He reckons that fox is getting wilier and braver. I'm not sure our picnic did the trick, Chipstick. There weren't any fox prints near the food, and half of it was still there this morning.'

I hoped the garden really was as quiet as Grandad

said. I straightened my colander and picked up my frying pan.

'Best keep your wits about you, Chipstick,' Grandad said, patting my back and making my breastplate clang. 'Just in case.'

As I ventured past the apple trees I kept my eyes wide open, scanning the borders and rows of vegetables.

Zing flew above me, flitting back and forth but always staying close. He looked as on edge as I felt.

But so far so quiet.

The sun glinted off my baking-tray breastplate and tin-foil helmet and I could almost imagine I was a knight. I readied my frying-pan shield and advanced on the dragon-fruit tree.

And then I caught a glimpse of orange through the spiky leaves. Not knowing whether to run towards it or away, one leg chose to investigate and the other tried to flee. Which left me lurching to the ground.

As the clang of the metal baking trays hitting the

ground reverberated around the garden, a shot of flame blasted out from the tree. With lightning reflexes honed from dealing with Flicker's sparks in the early days, I whipped the frying pan up to protect my face and then scrabbled away, hoping I'd be out of range of a second blast.

I ducked behind the wheelbarrow and peered out to see the orange dragon eyeing me fiercely as it thumped the ground with both its tails. Zing suddenly zapped to my side and the dragon paused in its tail beating, eyes flicking from me to Zing, before it twisted away and flew towards Jim's garden.

As it passed the hen coop, one of the hens spotted it and started clucking madly and flapping its wings and two more chickens rallied to its defence. The orange dragon was startled at the feathery attack and backed away, only to catch one of its tails on the little wire fence between the gardens. Being caught on the fence threw it into a panic and it wriggled wildly until it managed to get free and then flew off, bashing into several runner-bean frames on its way. They tumbled to the ground as the dragon darted into the depths of the dragon-fruit tree, scorching a dangly leaf as it went.

I winced. I'd always thought the tendrils on the tree looked a bit like a burst of flames, but at this rate they might actually burst into flames.

The clucking hens had brought Jim racing to their rescue and I heard him from the other side of the coop, cooing and shushing.

'There, there, you three, what's been ruffling your feathers?' He scooped one of them up and stalked around the coop. He peered over the fence, suddenly spotting me.

'All right, Tomas?' he said.

There was a time when he'd have gone beetroot red and started yelling at me, blaming me for his het-up hens. But we were past all that.

'Did you see what got them all of a flap?' he asked. 'Poor Melody,' he added stroking the chicken's feathers. 'She's beside herself.'

I shook my head.

'I bet it was that fox again.' He wrinkled his nose and sniffed the air. 'Smelly thing. I saw a glimpse of orange disappearing out the back hedge when I said goodnight to the hens yesterday. But surely it wouldn't have the nerve to come snooping in broad daylight?'

He scowled, then examined the ground. 'Can't see any paw prints or scratchings,' he said. 'Must be one cunning fox.'

I suddenly remembered what Grandad had said about there not being any fox prints near the picnic. No fox prints anywhere. I looked again at the mess the dragon had just caused. And the smell we had noticed over by the shed and that now lingered in the air around me and Jim. And the penny finally dropped. This had never been the work of a fox. The mess, the frightened hens, the stinkiness – it was all the orange dragon. It looked like as well as blasting out fire it unleashed a blast of stink when it was cornered.

'You all right, Tomas? You look like you just swallowed a fly.'

I nodded quickly.

The orange dragon was not exactly flying under the radar. What if after all this time Jim discovered our secret? That we weren't just growing runner beans and raspberries, we were growing dragons!

I needed to find a way to send this fiery dragon on its way north – and fast!

ORANGE DRAGON

Type: Unknown

Physical characteristics:
Horned head, collar of
spikes, spines on back,
two orange tails
with pincers.

Diet: Unknown

Special skills: To be confirmed but
unleashes stink when alarmed, which is a
pretty good defence mechanism.

Dragonality: Unfriendly, combative.

Warning: Danger of fire blast. Can use
pincer tails for double attack.

18
How to Scare
a Dragon

When Grandad joined me a bit later, we had to take it in turns to be on dragon watch. One kept an eye out for surprise attacks, while the other got on with digging and clearing the mess. It definitely wasn't as relaxing as usual in the garden. The trouble was, the orange dragon kept darting around and so our efforts to stay out of its way – and out of range – weren't going very well. Grandad was getting jumpier by the second.

'If it'd just settle in one place,' he said, 'then maybe we could rub along.'

'I think it's disappeared into that tree,' I replied. 'Let's hope it stays there.'

But the next second it shot out of the cover of the apple tree, sending a couple of pigeons flapping in panic. We both ducked as a burst of flames rocketed past us as the dragon zoomed over our heads and disappeared behind the shed.

'How about a peace offering?' I said. 'Maybe if we put something out for it to eat, it'll know we're friend not foe.'

'It's worth a try,' Grandad agreed.

I tentatively laid one of Nana's jam tarts, an apple, a stick of celery and a fairly hairy marshmallow on the ground and stepped back.

A few moments later the orange dragon dived down, turned the marshmallow into a blackened ball with one fiery blast and batted the jam tart into the air so pastry and jam splattered against the shed. It took the stick of celery in its claws and I thought we had success, until it dropped it unceremoniously into the water butt.

'Doesn't look like this one's a fan of Nana's cooking,'

Grandad said, eyeing the sticky mess on the shed.

'I guess not.'

'Think it might be time for a spot of lunch for us,' Grandad said, wiping his forehead, 'and a calming cup of tea. What do you say?'

I glanced round to the back of the shed and, spotting an orange pincer about to lob a clump of compost at me, nodded.

DRAGON EATING HABITS

It's good to figure out as quickly as possible what your dragon likes to eat and keep them well supplied.

Flicker likes anything green and leafy and especially loves broccoli and my cheese plant — which isn't

actually made of cheese. But Zing hadn't liked anything I'd offered him, not even jam kippers. It took me a while to realise he was charging up like a battery, feeding off the electrical energy of my remote-control helicopter, the radio and even lemons!

You might be lucky and have a dragon like Sunny who basically eats anything – or everything actually, which is less helpful. (It also has explosive results – Sunny has turbo-boosting farts like you wouldn't believe. Good luck if your dragon takes after Sunny! Ted had to quickly learn to hide his snacks and time Sunny's meals so he could point his back end out the window afterwards.)

On the way up to the house a message came through from Liam.

> **_Liam_**
>
> **Hey, Tomas**
>
> **How's the fox-foiling plan going? Do you think it's dangerous to be this bored? I feel like my brain cells are dying off from lack of stimulation. Lucky Aura, hey! Imagine going on a proper expedition into the rainforest. She just messaged to tell me that last night after a day on the boat they set up camp by the river. Arturo told stories by the fire and she went to sleep leaning against Dreki with howler monkeys screeching. She had a dream about hacking her way through the forest with a machete and finding the dragon-fruit tree. Do you think they really will find it?**

Tomas

I dunno. It's hard to see how if Arturo hasn't found it after all this time. I wish I was there though!

False alarm on the fox. Turns out it was the fiery dragon all the time! How can I get it to leave the garden? It keeps attacking us, and at this rate Jim's going to find out we're growing dragons!

Liam

Can Zing show it the way?

Tomas

Zing tried to make friends, but when he zapped over to it the dragon nearly fried him to a crisp. He won't go near it now.

Liam

Have you tried scaring it off?

Tomas

Not really. I think we're more scared of it than it is of us.

Liam

I've heard of bird scarers. Could you make a dragon scarer? That way at least you won't be the ones facing any fiery outbursts.

Tomas

Hey, that might work. Thanks!

It felt good to have a plan, and with Grandad's help I was sure I could come up with the Ultimate Dragon Scarer. I asked him when we were clearing up from lunch.

'The bird scarers farmers use are made to look like predator birds,' he said, handing me a plate to dry.

'They're kites and the shadows they cast across the field frighten the smaller birds away. But I don't expect this dragon'll be scared off by seeing a dragon shape. I mean, the little dragons have never been alarmed when Flicker and Sunny and the rest of them have been in the garden. And just think of the size of them in comparison. I wonder what would scare it?'

I reached up to put the plate on the shelf and suddenly an image of the dragons Kat had told me about flew into my mind. Dragons that loved water.

'Well, it's a fire dragon, I said, 'so I bet it wouldn't like meeting a water dragon. That would be bound to scare it off.'

'Now that is good thinking, Chipstick. Although how exactly are you planning on making one of those?'

The great thing about Grandad is that he always encourages me to think outside the box; to invent and to try and to not mind if it all goes wrong along the way. I'm full of ideas and he's full of know-how so, between us, we always make a brilliant team.

I tapped the side of my nose and grinned.

'I'm going to need that box you're always telling me to think outside of.'

By the end of the afternoon we had our water-dragon scarer. We'd done a pretty good job on the body and head, using some big cardboard boxes that Grandad's strimmer and new garden tools had come in. We'd even cut out some jagged teeth and I'd painted on two fierce eyes. And we'd shaped some wings that I could flap using bits of string.

'I think the beast is ready,' Grandad said, standing back to admire the spines he'd just stuck along its back.

I stood next to him, my hands covered in blue paint, feeling pretty proud of our mighty dragon.

I just hoped that my idea to run the hose out of its mouth so that it looked like it was breathing sprays of water would add some majesty.

19
Into the Dragon's Mouth

'Let's see what our fiery friend thinks of it, shall we?' Grandad said as he lifted up the water dragon and set off with it down the garden. I clanked my way behind, fully suited in armour again.

He laid the dragon on the grass under the tree, gave me a hearty slap on my metallic back and said, 'Soon as you see it, point our beast in its direction, give me a wave to turn on the tap and then get yourself out of range quick smart.'

I nodded and tried to stop clanking with nerves as I scanned the garden for signs of orange.

For a while we both stood, sentries poised at

opposite ends of the garden, and then Grandad went off to get a chair and a paper to read. With no sign of the dragon, I let the breath I'd been holding out and began to wonder if it had finally flown off. But then, just as we'd let our guard down, I saw it fly out from the dragon-fruit tree.

I started waving at Grandad, who leaped up and hurried over to the tap. He gave me a thumbs up and I aimed the hose. Nothing happened, no water spurted from the dragon's mouth . . . and then I realised the nozzle on my end needed opening. I reached into the dragon's mouth and fumbled with the hose, leaping back as water gushed out. I stood dripping as the force of the water whipped the hose into a frenzy, making it weave about like an angry snake. The dragon's head, attached to it, twisted wildly and for a second I cheered silently, thinking this must surely scare the orange dragon away. But then I saw that all the water was soaking into the cardboard.

Within moments the water dragon was a soggy mess, one of its wings sagging to the ground and the other torn right off by another twist of the hose. Blue paint trickled away into the grass.

The orange dragon, which had settled on a branch, stared down. I signalled to Grandad to turn off the tap and gingerly backed away.

As I did, the orange dragon flew down and began nudging the water dragon's limp wing with its snout. It turned to face me and let out an angry burst of flame that sent me skittering away. With a last look at the bedraggled blue ex-dragon the orange dragon disappeared back into the dragon-fruit tree.

'Time for plan B,' Grandad said as he helped me carry the soggy boxes back to the house.

'I wish it didn't keep disappearing into the dragon-fruit tree,' I said. 'How am I going to get close enough to water the roots? And it's due a sprinkling of ash. But I can't do that without risking a flame attack. I might

be able to jump out the way, but what if it scorches the tree?'

'Not to worry, Chipstick. I'm sure we'll come up with something. Our heads are like this garden. If we sprinkle them with the seeds of the things we know, all sorts of wonderful things might start growing in them, things we never even planted. That's how I imagine ideas pop up. They're like magic blooming flowers.' He grinned.

'I think my garden might just be a tangle of weeds,' I said.

'And that's exactly why it needs a bit of space and looking after,' he replied, ruffling my hair. 'Got to look after the garden in your head just as carefully as this one right here.' And he paused to sniff one of his roses.

When I got home, I found Lolli's door closed. I gently pushed it open and peered in. Lolli was standing with her back to me. She was wearing one of Mum's dresses that trailed along the carpet.

'Hey, Lollibob,' I said, hoping she'd forgiven me for leaving her behind.

She turned her head and then, holding onto the table, slowly turned the rest of her body, wobbling as she did so. As I stepped across the room, I realised that either I'd shrunk or Lolli had had a serious growth spurt while I'd been out.

She took a step towards me and then paused, a look of fierce concentration on her face. The next step was less successful, and I lunged forward to catch her as she wobbled, buckled and fell.

'What are you doing?' I laughed, trying to hold her up as she wriggled crossly in my arms.

I plonked her down on the edge of the bed. Sadly, she lifted the hem of the dress and I saw two plastic tubs sellotaped to her feet.

'I wanna be big,' she whispered. 'Then I can do flying too.'

I sat down next to her and gave her a squeeze.

'You do all the fun things,' she said grumpily.

I thought about everyone else off having adventures and how that made me feel. At least I went flying with Flicker, even if it was only round our village. Lolli hadn't even got to do that.

Just then Mr Floppybobbington, Lolli's rabbit, hopped out from under the bed and an image flashed into my mind of her in the garden with him.

'Hold on a minute,' I said, and leaped off the bed.

I started fishing around in her toy box until I'd found what I was looking for, then held it up triumphantly.

'Maybe we could make something like this,' I said.

Lolli's face didn't immediately light up with excitement as I'd hoped. I looked down at the baby carrier in my hand which Lolli often wore strapped to her chest. Two brown bear ears were only just visible over the edge of it. I positioned the teddy a bit higher so he could see out. 'I mean, we'll make it so you can see obviously,' I explained. 'I can wear it, and you'll be safe as houses while we're flying.'

I stood there grinning, feeling very proud of my brilliant idea, but instead of jiggling and dancing about, Lolli glared at me.

'I'm not a baby,' she said crossly, and ripping the plastic tubs off her feet she swept out of the room, except it wasn't really a sweep because the dress was so long she kept standing on it, until she ended up crawling awkwardly on her hands and knees, which probably didn't help her to feel big.

I stood watching her go, feeling like a deflating balloon. All in all it had been a day of failed ideas.

20
Ambushed!

Over the next few days things didn't get any better. Thanks to the superhero squad pooling ideas, I'd had plans B, C, D and E, but they'd all resulted in an F for failure. I'd tried banging pots and pans to scare the dragon away, and playing loud music. I'd flashed lights and sprayed water. I'd even downloaded the sound of a walrus and bellowed that out, hoping it might sound like a terrifying monster. But the dragon still refused to leave and all I'd done was make Jim moan at us for disturbing his hens.

I'd run out of ideas and was getting as jumpy as Grandad in the garden. And because I'd been so busy throwing ideas at the orange dragon, I hadn't had any left for the guide, so I'd done nothing on that either.

On Friday I woke sweating from one of those dreams that leave you feeling like you've just run a marathon dressed as a chicken. I'd been stumbling around a tangled forest, searching the undergrowth, desperate to find something. A dragon or an idea or both. I could hear Aura calling from somewhere, but my machete was a banana so I couldn't cut through to get to her. I was actually relieved when the banana grew wings and flew off, taking me with it.

After breakfast I sat at my desk and watched Zing hopping across the floor. He'd been wriggling about under my bed and had come out with two socks stuck to his scales. I leaned down and pulled them off. It wasn't very dignified having a holey sock on your head. He flew up and joined me, little flecks of silver shooting across his wings.

'Lolli wants to fly,' I said, exasperated. 'This dragon could end up setting the dragon-fruit tree on fire. And I am all out of ideas.'

My shoulders sagged and Zing landed on my lap and looked up at me, his lightning bolt tail gently tapping my leg.

'It's OK,' I said, rubbing his head. 'It's just all a bit hard at the moment.'

I felt a familiar buzz of energy as my hair stuck up and I smiled down at him.

'Don't worry, I won't give up,' I reassured him.

One thing I'd learned from Grandad and from growing dragons was that things weren't always easy. But you still had to keep trying.

WHAT I'VE LEARNED FROM GRANDAD

Friends and families stick together like the very best sticky jam tarts.

Be kind. You don't know what's going on for other people. Even if someone's being grumpy, try and fight fire with friendliness. Find the kind and you never know what else you'll find.

Slow down. There's always time to stop and smell the roses — however busy and complicated life gets.

Be patient. Things take time. And change is OK (even if it doesn't always feel like it). If nothing changed, nothing would grow, and everything needs to grow, even us.

Talk. Having a natter can really help, especially if there's a cup of tea and one of Nana's ginger biscuits with it.

Look after the small things. Even slugs.

Just as I was about to head downstairs a message popped up.

Kat to Tomas, Ted, Liam and Aura
I was right! We were being watched! We went back to check on the tree, and while we were there one of the fruit started glowing. Just as the dragon burst out, we were ambushed!

I stared at the words. Then waited, heart racing, to see if there was going to be another message. Ambushed by who? Were the twins OK? And what about the new baby dragon?

Kat

Sorry, Kai knocked my arm and I pressed send before I'd finished.

Someone grabbed the dragon and then grabbed us. I thought my heart was going to explode out my face.

Hey, can we video chat? You need to see this for yourselves.

It looked as if it was only me joining the call. I sat staring at the screen, waiting for their faces to pop up. And then nearly fell backwards off my chair. Because it wasn't their faces! Instead of Kat and Kai joining me on the call, there were three people I'd never seen in my life. They were beaming at me, but I was so surprised and confused I just gazed blankly back. Then my eyes flicked to the little dragons that perched on their shoulders.

The next second Kat and Kai's grinning faces joined

them and they all scooched in close to fit everyone in view.

'So,' Kat said, her eyes sparkling, 'you're not going to believe this, but it looks like we're not the only superhero squad!!'

21
Zaoan from the Superhero Squad

'*Zaoan*, Tomas. I'm Luan and this is my brother Liang and my friend Meilin.'

Liang waved and grinned and Meilin smiled and nodded. As she did, the little blue dragon on her shoulder stretched its neck and tapped its head on her cheek. She reached up and gently tapped its head back.

'Bao is pleased to meet you too,' she said. 'He must like the look of you, because usually he camouflages himself when he sees anyone new. He's an expert at not being seen.'

'Like Dodger,' Kai said. 'Except Bao's scales turn reflective like little mirrors. It's so cool!'

As they spoke, Liang was jiggling away on the end. He suddenly blurted out excitedly, 'I was born the year of the dragon so that makes me the leader!'

'It doesn't,' Luan said quickly, shaking her head.

The emerald dragon that had been perched on Liang's shoulder suddenly flew up and started circling their heads. I noticed Luan's dragon keeping a wary eye on it.

'See, Min agrees!' Liang declared happily. 'She's on my side.'

'There are lots of dragon-fruit trees where we live,' Luan said, ignoring her brother. 'Most of them just grow fruit, but last year we found one that actually grew dragons! And until we met Kat and Kai we thought it was the only one in the world. We didn't want them finding out the secret so we ambushed them.'

'We're really sorry about that,' Meilin said quickly. 'Especially as it turned out they knew about the dragons already!'

'I'm not sorry,' Liang said fiercely. 'We promised to protect the dragons and that's what we were doing. Anyway, it wasn't even a proper ambush, not after Luan sneezed.' He scowled at his sister.

'Kai's told us about the guide you're writing,' Luan went on. 'And that you'd like to know a bit more about dragons in China?'

'That'd be brilliant,' I said.

As she spoke, the dragon on her shoulder stretched out its wings proudly. The scales on its body were turquoise and its wings shimmered all different colours as if someone had thrown glitter over them.

'This is Xin,' Luan said. 'Her name means "beautiful". And she knows it!'

Kai suddenly piped up, 'If you want to put her name in the guide, it's said "Shin", but you write it X-i-n.'

I gave him a thumbs up.

'It's so great to meet you all,' I said.

At that moment Zing flew down and hovered in

front of me. 'And this is Zing,' I said, and laughed as he flared silver, vanished and then reappeared on top of my head.

'Hello, a-ma-zing Zing!' Luan chuckled.

'I can do something brilliant for your guide,' Liang said. 'I want to write about Longmen. I know a lot about the Dragon Gate. It's amazing! There's a legend that says that fish called carp are able to leap over this gate and become dragons. Some people think you can find this gate at Jiulong Waterfalls, also called Nine Dragon Waterfalls. When I'm older I'm going to find the Dragon Gate. Kat has told us how the legend you read was wrong – well, imagine if there was more to the gate than the legend says. What if it's actually a portal and that's how the dragons travel between places?'

Liang had been getting more and more excited as he spoke. And as he revved up so did Min, darting back and forth above them, making Meilin duck every time she circled overhead. As Min rocketed past Liang's face he laughed and leaned back so far he wobbled off his chair. He picked himself up, still giggling while Luan moved closer to the screen and whispered, 'He's got a very good imagination. I'm not so sure about magic gates.'

I smiled along, but I have to admit that I was as excited as Liang. As soon as he'd said the word 'portal', my own fizzing imagination had started working on hyperdrive!

Just at that moment Min dived down and shot across the screen, making everyone leap backwards yet again and sending a pot of pens flying. A burst of sparks erupted from her mouth and as she passed Bao she flicked him with her tail and sent the little dragon toppling off Meilin's shoulder. It didn't look like Min was going to settle any time soon. And even Liang was starting to look a bit worried.

'Sorry,' Luan said, with her arm shielding her head. 'Our dragon Baiyun was never this much trouble. She was the first dragon we grew, a cloud-white sky dragon. She still comes to visit us just like Crystal and Dodger have been visiting Kat and Kai. But this latest crop has got some really excitable ones.' She looked pointedly at Min, still zooming back and forth.

'Have you tried using ash?' I said.

Luan shook her head.

'It doesn't always work, but it might be worth trying.'

She suddenly ducked so low that she disappeared from view completely. As she popped up again there was a loud crash.

'I'm sorry, I think we'd better go,' she said as she watched Liang and Meilin hurrying away. 'She's heading downstairs.'

'I'll send you something,' I said quickly. 'I can write a bit for the guide. Maybe it'll help.'

'Brilliant, thanks, Tomas. And we'll send you something too! It was lovely to meet you.'

CHINESE DRAGONS

The Chinese dragon is known as the Long or Lung.

They have many forms like turtles and fish, but mainly they are like a snake with four legs. Mostly they don't have wings but can still fly from being magic. They represent prosperity and good luck.

Some of the dragons hatching from the dragon-fruit tree do have wings but some are like the Long and don't.

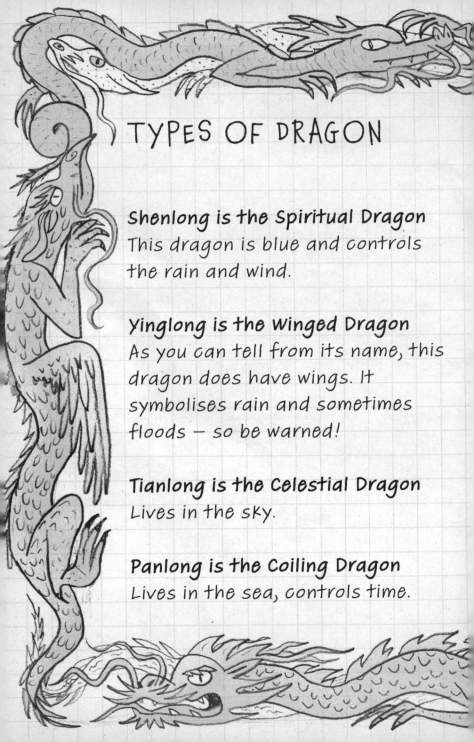

TYPES OF DRAGON

Shenlong is the Spiritual Dragon
This dragon is blue and controls the rain and wind.

Yinglong is the Winged Dragon
As you can tell from its name, this dragon does have wings. It symbolises rain and sometimes floods — so be warned!

Tianlong is the Celestial Dragon
Lives in the sky.

Panlong is the Coiling Dragon
Lives in the sea, controls time.

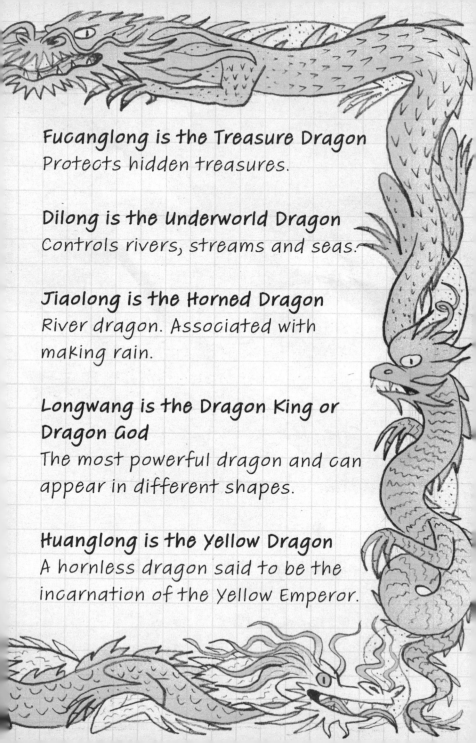

Fucanglong is the Treasure Dragon
Protects hidden treasures.

Dilong is the Underworld Dragon
Controls rivers, streams and seas.

Jiaolong is the Horned Dragon
River dragon. Associated with
making rain.

**Longwang is the Dragon King or
Dragon God**
The most powerful dragon and can
appear in different shapes.

Huanglong is the Yellow Dragon
A hornless dragon said to be the
incarnation of the Yellow Emperor.

Here's a picture of the first dragon we grew. She's called Baiyun. She is cloud-white and doesn't have wings. She can control water and rain. She is the fastest dragon you will ever meet.

22
Howl, Yowl, Hiss, Bang

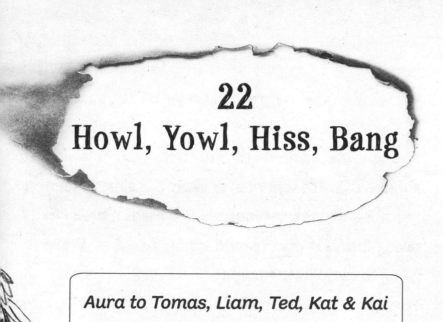

Aura to Tomas, Liam, Ted, Kat & Kai
We've reached the Hidden City!
This is AMAZING!!!!!!!!!!

We left the boat before sunrise yesterday, paddled all day in canoes and then had to trek FOUR hours through the rainforest!! I'm never complaining about walking to school ever again! I've already seen toucans and a howler monkey and loads more!! I'm taking loads of photos and doing sketches. We're going to camp here tonight!

Wish you were all here!

Aura

There were already a couple of replies from Ted and Liam, though it didn't look as if Kat and Kai had seen it yet.

Ted

Awesome! Did you know howler monkeys are the loudest animals in the world? What's the Hidden City like? Send us some pictures!

I wished I was there too! On the way to Nana and Grandad's I did pretend to battle my way through our front garden, which was about as overgrown as a rainforest. But a slug and a pigeon weren't quite as impressive to encounter. Although a hiss from Tomtom, who'd stalked out of the hedge, made me jump a mile, imagining some jungle jaguar. Heart hammering, I hurried onwards, Zing flapping overhead and Tomtom tracking us from a distance. I hadn't seen him at Nana and Grandad's the past few days and I wondered if maybe he'd had a run-in with the dragon and been keeping out of its way.

As I swung their gate open, I glanced back and saw

a flash of ginger fur leaping onto the fence and watched him nimbly disappear round the other side of the house. I hoped for both our sakes that the dragon had finally gone.

Passing the cold remains of Grandad's bonfire, I stopped to cram my pockets full of ash. I even filled a plant tray and held it above my head in the hope it would act as a sort of peace offering, if the dragon was still here.

As I neared the end of the garden, though, I saw Grandad crouching down and a blast of fire shooting

out towards the corner of Jim's hen coop, where the hens were clucking and flapping their wings in panic. I had a feeling this little dragon would be more interested in creating ash than in the sprinklings I had to offer.

DRAGON TRAINING

So you probably know by now that dragons are not pets — and some are a lot friendlier than others. The chances are they might just do as they please. But when we discovered that not just the dragon-fruit trees but the dragons themselves like ash, because of the volcanos they live near in the Land of the Far North, we used it to encourage them to learn a few commands.

I've realised that having a pocketful of ash is a bit like Grandad keeping a stash of caramel toffees up his sleeve. If I start flagging when I'm helping him dig in the garden, or I have a moan or am feeling like a squashed raisin on the bottom of a shoe, the toffee distracts me and reminds me that Grandad is keeping an eye out for me. Ash is the same — it's like keeping a treat up your sleeve.

Just hold some in your open palm and your dragon should come to you. They like to rub it into their scales like hippos and elephants do with mud! It's especially good if you use the same whistle or a call whenever you give them the ash, so you can get their attention in a hurry.

Grandad often has a bonfire in the garden so I'm chief ash collector for the superhero squad. I keep a tin of it in the shed, just like Elvi did, and whenever anyone gets low they can come and stock up.

Of course, not all dragons are that interested in ash. (I learned that when I met Zing!)

Seeing Tomtom balanced on the fence, the orange dragon left the chickens and flew straight at him. Tomtom lashed out with one paw and the dragon diverted. As it circled back around, an irate ginger furball sprang down from the fence, raced past me with an angry hiss and shot up the nearest tree. I wasn't sure being high up was the best idea when your enemy could fly and you couldn't!

The dragon wouldn't leave him alone though. However much Tomtom arched his back and hissed, it kept on flying between the branches, trying to get closer.

Suddenly there was a thunderous bang and the sky exploded in colour. Tomtom yowled and fled down the tree, and the orange dragon let out a furious curl of flame and rocketed away.

'Blasted fireworks,' Jim shouted angrily, hurrying down his garden. He started cooing to the hens and making reassuring shushing noises. 'Every time I think they've used them all up, another one goes off.'

'They must have had some left over from that party the other night,' Grandad said.

'Why they bother letting them off in the middle of the afternoon is anyone's guess,' Jim replied. He frowned, eyeing the grey sky over the back hedge. Sure enough, a moment later another firework screamed its ascent and then burst into a fountain of purple. We all waited, braced for another whistling shriek or bang, but it seemed that was the last of them, for now anyway.

'Finally,' Jim grumped, and stomped back up his garden.

I found Tomtom shaking round the back of the shed. He hissed at me crossly as I reached to bring him out. I quickly drew back. It looked like I'd need something to tempt him. And I'd better find it quick as the orange dragon was perched on the shed roof, peering down at us. And it did not look happy.

23
Peace at Last

Usually I'd coax Tomtom out with a treat, but the only thing left in Grandad's secret stash of goodies was a rock-hard flapjack and he just hissed angrily when my hand came towards him with that.

'He's going to get a fiery shock if we don't get him out of there quick,' I said, eyeing the orange dragon, who was thumping its tail against the shed roof.

'You want a bit of catnip,' Grandad said. 'That'll do the trick.'

He hurried over to a large pot with purple flowers and picked a handful of leaves.

'Give this a go,' he said passing the bunch to me,

one eye still on the dragon. 'I grew it for cough mixture and bug spray, but cats love the stuff. Quick whiff of this and you'll have a happy, relaxed Tomtom.'

He was right. As Tomtom enjoyed the catnip, I was able to reach in and lift him out. There wasn't even his customary growly yowl.

'That's amazing,' I said, giving Tomtom a stroke. 'I can't remember the last time he let me get this close. It's nice.' I nestled my face into his fur. He was so soft.

'I reckon this garden's always got the answer,' Grandad replied with a wink.

I put Tomtom down on the ground gently and watched as he curled up where he was, too blissed out to even move. And then the strangest thing happened. The orange dragon, who had been watching us the whole time, flew down. But instead of blasting us with flames, it flapped over to the pot of purple flowers and started tearing off some leaves with its mouth. It flew over to Tomtom and laid them by his side. Then it went

back and forth and back and forth, until it'd laid a ring of green around the sleepy cat.

When the circle was complete, the dragon landed and cautiously hopped closer to Tomtom. The cat opened his eyes, but this time there was no hiss.

The orange dragon curled up next to my tiger-hearted cat and, the next thing we knew, they were both fast asleep.

'Well, there's a rum 'un,' Grandad said. 'What's going on there then?'

I realised we were both scratching our chins in confusion. Thoughts started fizzling in my head, like the fizzing fireworks. And then one exploded, a bright burst of genius lighting up my brain.

'What if our little dragon imprinted on a certain grumpy furball?' I exclaimed. 'That'd explain why it hasn't left. It's been looking for Tomtom. It wasn't trying to attack him, it was just trying to get close to him.'

'They've definitely both got a fiery temper,' Grandad said.

I paused, remembering the list of important things Grandad had taught me that I'd included in the guide. Grandad had always given Jim the benefit of the doubt, seeing past gruff old Grim, as I used to call him. There was usually a reason why people got grumpy. Maybe there was a reason this little dragon was so quick to flare into flames.

'Imagine bursting out of your fruit and coming face to face with a hissing ball of fury,' I said. 'That's bound to make you jumpy. And then there were those fireworks on its first night here. We know how scared Tomtom is of them. I bet it was just as terrified and copied what he did.'

It suddenly felt like I'd swallowed a stone which sat cold and heavy in my stomach. 'And then I spent all that time trying to scare it even more.'

I crouched down and, remembering the way Aura had calmed her dragon Rosebud when she got a fright, I gently blew over the little dragon's scales.

'I'm sorry I scared you,' I whispered. The dragon opened its eyes. I slowly reached out my hand and ran a finger down its spiky spine.

'Friends?'

There was a harmony of purring rumbles as both dragon and cat breathed out a long, contented sigh. As the dragon's tummy rose and fell I could see its scales were layered and the ones underneath glinted like amber in sunlight.

I smiled, relieved. 'Welcome to our garden, Amber,' I said.

The little dragon curled her tail around my wrist.

'I think she's happy with her name,' I said, glancing up at Grandad.

'Definitely,' he replied. 'Looks like you're quite the dragon whisperer,' he added with a grin.

~~ORANGE DRAGON~~
AMBER

Type: Still to discover

Physical characteristics:
Horned head, collar of
spikes, spines on back, two
orange tails with pincers.

Diet: Still need to find out!

Special skills: Can unleash stink
when alarmed.

Dragonality: ~~Unfriendly, combative,~~
Clever, loyal, caring, fiercely protective.

Warning: If startled may be danger of fire
blast. Can use pincer tails for
double attack.

24
Keep Those
Eyes Open

When I got home there was another message from Aura
waiting for me.

> **Aura**
> Rainforests are loud! I'm taking lots of videos to
> show you when I get back. Here I am in the Hidden
> City!! Do you recognise this wall?

I stared at the photo she'd attached, amazed to see my friend standing in the forest, her hand resting on the same ruin that Elvi had stood by. She'd staged the photo to be an exact match of the one I had of Elvi. And Aura was even giving the same grin as Elvi, the one that made you think she'd dropped a centipede down your back and was dying to tell you.

> **Aura**
>
> It's so frustrating, Tomas. I know the tree is here somewhere, I can feel it. But we could be really close and still not see it in all this forest. I so want to find it for Arturo.

The next picture showed Arturo sitting by a campfire. He was looking across at Aura, who was holding Rosebud up to a flower. He was watching her, smiling broadly, and it reminded me of the way Grandad looked at me.

208

ROSEBUD

Type: Flower dragon

Physical characteristics:
Bright green scales,
darker green wings shaped like ovals
with veins running through like
leaves, tiny spines on tail like
thorns, long horns which glow.

Diet: Plants and vegetables.

Special skills: Breath can make
flowers bloom. Green gas emitted
from other end makes everyone giggly.

Dragonality: Mischievous, fun, caring.

Warning: If alarmed will curl into ball on
nearest plant, where petal-like wings
make her hard to spot, but if you
get too close she'll use her thorned
tail to warn you off!

Liam to Tomas and Ted

You were right, Tomas, you've got to keep your eyes wide open. This holiday just got a whole lot less boring. Dad keeps dragging us round these Suffolk churches to look at paintings yaaaaawwwwn. But one church had this brilliant one of a dragon! And after that I kept spotting little stone dragon heads on walls and buildings everywhere. And then we found this! It's huge. It's carved out from the chalk on the hill.

There's this legend about a dragon terrorising the local village. They fought it and it disappeared into the marshes. I'm glad they didn't kill it! It just goes to show there are dragons everywhere!

Ted
Awesome!

Tomas
That's so cool!

Ted
Have you seen these?

I scrolled through the photos Ted had attached. There were some that just looked like a bunch of lines and shapes. But there was also a giant spider, a hummingbird,

a dog, a cat and some birds. They were carved into the landscape like Liam's dragon and looked enormous. Some must have been hundreds of metres long.

Liam
WOW!

Ted
They're called geolyphs. They were made thousands of years ago by people scraping away pebbles to reveal the soil underneath. You can find them all over the world. But these ones are called the Nazca Lines, they're in Peru. I just looked yours up, Liam — I think your dragon's pretty new. It was only carved in 2012. Cool, hey!

Tomas

Very! But why are they there?

Ted

Don't think anyone really knows. They're still discovering new ones too – lots of them you can only see from the air.

Liam

Just think what else might be out there! Who knows what we're missing right under our noses. My eyes are staying wide open from now on.

Ted

So how are things in the garden? Liam told me the fox was a red herring?

I laughed, imagining a furry-tailed fox with a fish head and fins.

Tomas

A lot better! Turns out Tomtom's not the best role model. The little dragon imprinted on the wrong hissing furball and learned a lot about being scared of everything – and leaping to attack mode. But I think we're all friends now. Which is just as well because you don't want to be on Amber's fiery side, believe me!

Ted sent over a sketchy drawing of Amber riding on Tomtom's back and I sent them both my doodle of the fish fox and we agreed to catch up the next day.

Over tea I showed Mum and Dad the photos Aura had sent and the ones of the geolyphs.

'I'm gonna make a joliff in the garden,' Lolli said, jumping up excitedly.

'I'm not sure you'd see it very clearly in our jungle,' Dad said with a laugh.

Lolli flopped down on the floor and Pea, who had been enjoying some honey, paused and flew over and landed on her tummy.

'I see Pea is feeling better,' I said.

Lolli nodded and looked down happily at the dragon. He was stuck with sticky honey legs to Lolli's jumper like a shiny brooch.

She lifted a finger and tickled the dragon's teeny snout and then whispered, 'Maybe I can get sticky like Pea and then I wouldn't fall off.'

'Fall off what?' Mum asked.

But Lolli didn't reply.

I knew what she meant though. Poor Lolli. She was still desperate to fly.

Zing settled between us and in unison our hair all stuck up, and even Lolli couldn't stop a giggle from wriggling its way out.

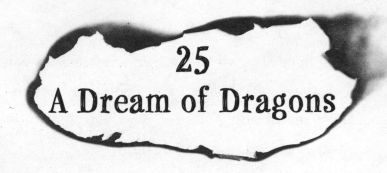

25
A Dream of Dragons

When Flicker was small, he'd curl up next to me when I went to bed and it was like having a scaly hot water bottle. Zing was more of a fidget. He'd start off lying near my feet and then the next second I'd hear him scratching away under the bed before a moment later he'd appear on my head, claws digging into my forehead.

As I got into bed though, he flew down and settled on my tummy, stretching his wings over me. I lay still, not wanting him to zap away too soon. I imagined what he'd be like fully grown and pictured him and Flicker flying side by side. I wondered if he still had wers to show me. Flicker had surprised me with his weather-controlling abilities long after I thought I knew everything about him. After a little while, I drifted off to sleep with him still there.

I dreamed of flying again, but this time I was looking down on a desert where a giant spider crawled its way across the land. It reached the outline of a hummingbird, which lifted from the ground and soared upwards and we followed it towards a vast forest.

As we flew on, Flicker's red wings shimmered against a great green rippling ocean of trees. Zing was perched between Flicker's horns, his lightning-bolt tail flaring silver and making the air crackle. In response Flicker opened his mouth and blew out an arc of sparks.

Suddenly I heard a roaring rumble and turned to see a slender dragon with four pink wings like a dragonfly's racing up behind us. Aura sat astride Dreki's back, Rosebud clinging to her arm like a bud on a branch. Dreki's ruby eyes sparkled as they flew past us

Up ahead, the river gushed over a great horseshoe-shaped waterfall. A mist of steam rose from the gaping cavern below.

'Like smoke from a dragon's mouth!' Liam cried.

Suddenly images of blackened lava fields and rice terraces that looked like scales flickered into my mind. From geolyphs to natural landmarks, the world was full of dragons!

'Maybe the river's not a snake – maybe it's a dragon and this is its head!' I cried.

'Except it has no wings,' Liam called back.

'Not all dragons have wings,' Meilin reminded him.

'That's right,' Aura cried. 'Remember Quetzalcoatl too!' and, laughing, she swooped around us.

Flicker's scales started changing colour and for some reason an image of Amber flashed into my mind. Not a fox and not an angry dragon. I just hadn't seen the whole picture, until I'd paused and stepped back to really look.

I urged Flicker to fly higher so I could I take it all in properly.

I let out the breath I'd been holding and cried out to the others to join me. Because, as I stared down, I knew that I really was looking at a vast forest dragon. From its twisting tail to its roaring head, where the river that burst onwards from its mouth licked the trees like a flickering tongue. And I could see now that the clearings I'd spotted spread out in curling lines either side of the river.

'They're like the feathers on Quetzalcoatl!' I hollered.

As our voices rose in excitement, our dragons flew faster, circling each other as they spiralled up and down in a swirling aerial dance.

Aura cupped her hands to her mouth and shouted, 'This dragon is here for a reason. It's here to show us the way to the tree, I just know it.'

'It is!' Liang shouted back. 'Remember how our

dragons go looking for water. Look at this dragon's tongue!'

I followed where he was pointing and saw that the flickering tongue of the great forest dragon was shimmering with glinting colours. The colours of dragon scales and feathers! And I watched as dragon after dragon rose up from the sparkling water to join us.

I woke up buzzing, with Zing hopping around on my chest. Sunlight sparkled through the window, keeping the vivid images of my dream alight. Every atom of me wanted to be there, soaring over that emerald forest with its rainbow of dragons hidden within it.

And then Lolli flew into the room, arms spread wide, and leaped onto the bed.

'I wanna fly,' she pleaded.

'I know. But try not to fly off the bed and crash-land,' I said.

'But I flied really high last night and didn't fall, not

ever.' She plonked herself down next to me. 'I really wanna.'

Then she added sulkily, 'I know it was only a dream, but if I can do it in my dream, I can do it. Promise.' She looked at me, eyes wide. 'I don't have to go over the forest, I can just go here.' She pointed towards the window. 'In the village. I won't fall off and I won't get lost. Tinkle knows all the way there and back.'

I stared at her.

'Lolli, did you dream about flying over a forest last night?'

She nodded eagerly and her eyes sparkled.

Across the room, my computer suddenly pinged.

Ted
Home tomorrow! Do you want to meet up?
Had the weirdest dream last night.

There was also one from Aura that had arrived while I was asleep.

> ## Aura
> Going to bed soon. Must be tired. I fell asleep by the fire while Arturo was telling another story. I felt really bad, but he just laughed. I had this brilliant dream and I wish it had been true – you were all here and we were riding over the forest on our dragons! And Liam kept shouting about a dragon's head and then we saw all these dragons flying out of its mouth.

My fingers were suddenly shaking so much with excitement I could hardly type.

> ## Tomas to the superhero squad
> Weird question but what did you dream about last night?

A minute later their replies flew in.

Ted

I was flying on Sunny over this forest and being chased by a giant spider. But there was a forest dragon too. And I think we found the dragon-fruit tree. Why?

Kat and Kai

Wait, what? Us too!

Liam

Same! What's going on?

26
Magic Grows All Around Us

It was torture waiting for the time to tick by and for Aura to wake up. She was six hours behind us and would still be fast asleep. At least I'd had time to let my fingers stop shaking so I could type a proper message, explaining that we had all shared the same dream.

I'd shared dreams with Flicker before, but we'd never all shared one together. I knew then that all our dragons had joined in the search for the dragon-fruit tree by sharing their dreams with us! And from their aerial view we had seen what we couldn't see before. With Dreki there to fly her, surely now Aura and Arturo would find it.

I pictured the colourful dragons skimming across the water of the river and hoped with every fibre of my being that I was right.

The hours dragged by and messages pinged back and forth between us as we all tried to contain our excitement. But none of them came from Aura. Until at last one did.

> **Aura**
>
> Arturo says that magic grows all around us. And that in the forest it is especially bright. We all had the same dream. Can you believe it! And because of that we found what we've been searching for. We nearly didn't though! Watch the videos I'm sending and you can see for yourself. As Arturo said, 'It's worth the wait!'

I clicked on the first video and knew that across the world all the superhero squad were watching the same thing.

Aura was filming her and Arturo riding on the back of Dreki. He was laughing and pointing down at the winding river, the tail of the mighty forest dragon.

We watched them flying over the canopy and the gushing waterfall, searching for signs of the dragons and the tree. I felt their excitement and then their frustration as the time passed and there was no sign of either. Had it all just been a wonderful dream? We all so wanted the same thing; could it have simply been wishful thinking?

And then Arturo cried out, 'Look, there! The eye of the dragon!'

Aura spun the camera round and for a second there was just a blur and a flash of sky and scales and then, as her hand steadied again and the picture focused, I saw a ring of rocks by the edge of the waterfall. And there, in the very centre, was a bright burst of green shot through with flecks of colour that radiated out. The film clip ended.

I punched the air and let out a whoop so loud that everyone came running in.

'Have you found the tarantulas?' Mum asked hopefully.

I just shook my head and pointed to the screen. I clicked on the second video clip and we watched it, grinning.

Aura and Arturo were standing by a dragon-fruit tree. Arturo's eyes twinkled as he held up his hands to the camera, showing two tiny bright emerald dragons. And as Aura's beaming face turned to us, more and more shining shapes flickered around her, until the air was a bright blaze of glinting colours, shimmering wings and feathered scales.

27
Grand High Dragon Whisperer

Later, in Grandad's garden, I sat with him outside the shed, watching Amber flutter-hop over Tomtom's tail as he flicked it back and forth. My tiger-hearted cat was clearly enjoying the game as much as the little dragon.

'I think Tomtom'll be sad to see that one go,' Grandad said. 'I've never known him so playful.'

'Maybe she'll come back and visit,' I said. And then added, 'And perhaps Arturo can come too, one day.'

'Maybe by plane rather than by dragon though,' he said with a chuckle. 'He's a braver man than me. I love these dragons, but you wouldn't get me up there like he was in that video.'

'I'm glad he did though. If it hadn't been for Arturo's eagle eyes they might have missed the dragons and never found the tree,' I said.

'Well, I expect when you've kept your eyes open for as long as he has, you see more than most people ever do.'

'I wish I could have been there,' I said.

'Your time'll come, Chipstick.'

I sighed, wondering if that was true and if I'd ever have an adventure like Aura or Kat and Kai.

'How's that guide of yours coming along?' Grandad asked.

'I don't know,' I said flatly. 'I thought I'd have more of it done by now.'

'Well, you've had your hands full. And don't forget, you've got the whole of your superhero squad on the case now too. You might be surprised how much you can pull together.'

'That's another thing,' I said. 'I wanted to write the

ultimate guide. But it turned out I didn't know as much as I thought I did.'

'I reckon you know a lot more than you think. If you read between the lines you might see you've learned all sorts along the way. Not least how to be a dragon whisperer.' And he motioned to Amber and I remembered blowing across her scales and how she'd looked at me.

'But I didn't know anything at all about the dragons in China before I met Luan, Liang and Meilin. Or Quetzalcoatl in Mexico. There are probably dragons all over the world that I haven't even heard of. So there must be loads more still to find out.'

Grandad laughed. 'That's a good thing. Life's about learning. Things grow – even guides.'

HOW TO BECOME A DRAGON WHISPERER

LISTEN TO YOUR DRAGON

- Dragons can't talk but they can communicate. You just have to do whole listening, with your eyes, your ears and your heart.

USEFUL THINGS TO WATCH FOR:

- Dragons lower their heads when they are really listening to you.

- If a dragon disagrees with you, they might give you a quick flick with their tail. So if you're not sure they're going to like what you have to say, stand out of swiping distance.

- A hungry dragon will bob its head up and down.

- When a dragon moves in circles and scratches at the ground it is probably tired and getting ready to sleep.

- If a dragon is about to full-on attack, their shoulders will often hunch up. They may unleash warning sparks or smoke as a signal to back away. Folded wings will be unfurled to make them look bigger.

- Contented dragons often make a low rumble — a bit like a purr.

- Dragons greet each other by bending their heads forward and crossing necks, so each of them rests their head on the other's shoulders — this might be why baby dragons like to settle on your shoulder and curl their tail around your neck.

● Dragons sing to each other. If you're lucky enough to be around when they sing, you know they trust you.

I really hoped Grandad was right about the guide being OK. I laid out everything I had so far and pored over it, adding a few more details here and there.

Then I scanned the pages and sent them to everyone, asking if we could have a group chat the next day to talk about it.

Trying to find a time when the whole superhero squad could meet virtually meant doing some super-twisty maths. When we finally got together, I was munching on a lunchtime sandwich, Kat, Kai, Luan, Liang and Meilin had just finished their evening meal and Aura was about to have her breakfast!

'Where are Liam and Ted?' I asked.

'Maybe they got the time wrong?' Meilin suggested.

'But Liam's only in Suffolk!'

Just then Liam and Ted's faces popped up as if they had arrived together.

'Sorry I'm late,' Ted said, waving at everyone.

'Me too,' Liam added.

Seeing everyone there, I suddenly felt my stomach do a leaping somersault that landed really badly and almost took my breath away. What would they think of what I'd written?

There was an awkward pause as everyone waited for someone else to speak first. And then Luan, Liam and Ted all started to talk at once. Before they could even get out a couple of words, Liam's screen froze. He'd just leaned in and his mouth was wide open, filling the screen, and his eyes were even wider. We all fell about laughing and when he came back to us a second or two later he looked utterly bemused.

'Did I freeze again? Honestly, the connection here is prehistoric! I was just saying,' he continued, and then promptly froze again in another hilarious grimace. He returned just as quickly and rattled on, ignoring the rest of us as we tried and failed to stop laughing. 'I was just saying . . . how epic the guide is!'

'It really is,' agreed Kat.

'I loved the bit about looking after the tree,' Luan said.

'And I didn't know about that Draco the Dragon constellation!' Kai added. 'That's amazing!'

'Those flying tips were spot on,' put in Liam.

'Yeah,' Ted piped up. 'Guess you are Grand High DragonMaster after all!'

There was enthusiastic agreement from the others and a whooping cheer from Liang and I felt my stomach do another somersault, but this time it was definitely a happy one and landed like a champion who'd just won gold.

'You know,' I said, beaming, 'I think I like Grand High Dragon Whisperer better. And I couldn't have done any of it without the rest of you.'

'Or me,' Lolli said, barrelling up and flumping onto my lap. She peered at the screen and waggled a finger over everyone's face in turn. She spun it round to show me and I could see she'd drawn a little smiling face on the tip of her finger.

'No, or you,' I said giving her a squeeze.

She wriggled out of my grip. 'Careful, you're squishing Filbert.' And she wagged her finger at me sternly, although clearly Filbert wasn't bothered as he was still grinning.

'Can Filbert join the superhero squad?' she asked.

I glanced at the others. The superhero squad had certainly grown since the early days when Flicker was the only dragon we knew. And honestly, it had been the best fun.

'Absolutely!' I replied. 'The more the merrier.'

28
Sticky Lolli Bobalob

The next day I sat with Nana and Grandad in the garden having a cup of tea and a natter. Leaning back I watched two clouds racing across the sky. And then, seeing a shimmer of red through the grey, I laughed and pointed up.

'Sometimes even I can't spot him. It looks like Flicker and Tinkle are heading to the Dragons' Den. Can we go?'

Grandad nodded and got to his feet, waving at Lolli who was running down the path towards us.

'Up for an adventure, young Lollibob?' he asked, sweeping her up in his arms.

She nodded fiercely, keeping her eyes fixed on me as she clung to him. He began to twirl her round, like he did with me when I was smaller and it had felt like the nearest thing to flying. She flung her head back and whooped.

'We can go to the den now, but there are jobs in the garden we must do later,' Grandad said, letting her down. 'Everything's blooming at the moment, but it does need a bit of looking after.'

Hearing him say that reminded me of what he'd said about looking after the garden in our head and ideas blooming. Was there a seed planted in my mind that could bloom into the answer I needed to help Lolli fly?

We bundled into the back of Grandad's car and drove to the nature reserve where the dragons stayed now that they were big. And all the way, while Grandad and Lolli sang rhyming songs, I sat quietly, giving the garden in my head time to grow some new ideas.

When we got out of the car and stood looking across to the island, I couldn't help smiling.

Flicker and Tinkle appeared between the trees and flew across the water towards us. This was the closest Lolli had got to flying, sitting with me on Flicker as he ferried us across to the island in the middle of the reserve. She moved towards him, obviously determined to enjoy her one little chance to fly. But I pulled her back.

'I think it's time Lolli and Tinkle had a turn at flying,' I said.

She squealed and grabbed my hand, shaking it up and down in delight.

Grandad raised an eyebrow, but he waited for me to go on.

'I think I have a way to make sure you're safe,' I said. 'And you were the one that planted the seed of the idea, Lolli,' I went on, smiling at Grandad.

She looked at me quizzically.

'When you said you could get sticky like Pea, when he was stuck to your jumper with honey – remember?'

I motioned for Zing to join us. 'You know how Zing always has socks stuck to him when he's had a bit of lunch?'

Lolli nodded.

'Well, maybe you can be a sock!'

Now she looked really confused.

'With Zing's static charge, he can keep you stuck to Tinkle.'

Lolli jumped up and down and clapped her hands.

'Sticky Lolli Bobalob!' she cried.

Rising up into the air on Flicker's back always made my heart soar. But seeing Lolli's beaming face as she rose up on Tinkle next to me made it whoosh up to the stars in delight. With Zing attached to her, we swooped around the island, calling out to Grandad as he waved below. And when we finally landed and Zing let go, she tumbled from Tinkle's back, glowing and bright. Pea peeped out from her pocket and flew up to land on her nose.

Grandad wrapped an arm round me and I grinned up at him.

Then Flicker nudged my back and I turned. He brought his massive head lower and I stared into his diamond eyes, blinking as the colours danced and shone so brightly. My mind filled with the images of my dreams, red mud pools and gushing geysers, crashing waterfalls and a great volcano erupting with dragons, their colours exploding into the sky.

'It looks an exciting place to explore,' Grandad said, and I looked up and saw the same images twinkling in his eyes too.

'I think he wants to show me,' I said hopefully.

'I told you adventure was waiting for you,' he replied. 'And there's no one I'd trust more to share it with you.'

Grandad ran a hand along Flicker's scales as I

climbed up onto my dragon's back and then he patted my leg and gave me a wink.

'Are you ready?'

I grinned and nodded.

'Good. Then it's time to soar, Chipstick. It's time to soar!'

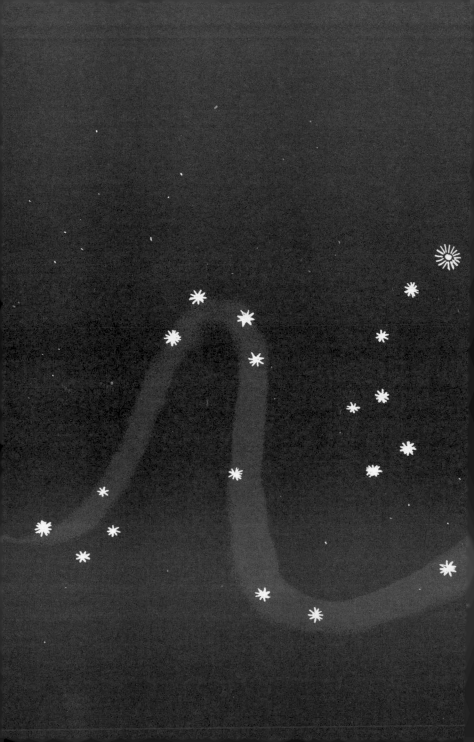

So there it is, our not-so-ultimate
guide. But that's OK, because Grandad's
right — even guides need to keep
growing. Dragons grow all over the
world, and there's still so much to
find out.

So now I need your help to grow
this guide.

There are some blank fact files here
for you to fill in your own dragon
details! Don't forget to write about
their special abilities and if there's
anything you should warn us about if
we meet them.

The more we know, the easier it will be to look after the dragons and keep them safe.

Are you ready to join the superhero squad?

Then grab your oven gloves and water pistols and keep your eyes wide, wide open! Because the magic is only just beginning.

Tomas

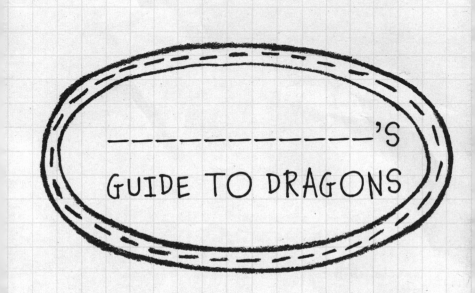

_____'S

GUIDE TO DRAGONS

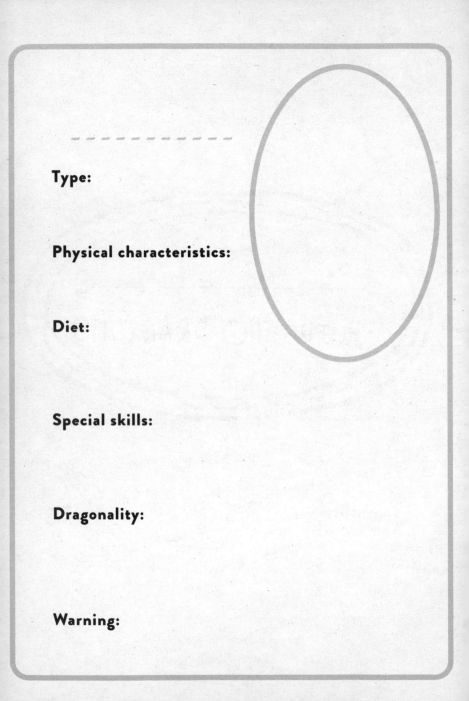

- - - - - - - - - -

Type:

Physical characteristics:

Diet:

Special skills:

Dragonality:

Warning:

Type:

Physical characteristics:

Diet:

Special skills:

Dragonality:

Warning:

Type:

Physical characteristics:

Diet:

Special skills:

Dragonality:

Warning:

Type:

Physical characteristics:

Diet:

Special skills:

Dragonality:

Warning:

Type:

Physical characteristics:

Diet:

Special skills:

Dragonality:

Warning:

- - - - - - - - - -

Type:

Physical characteristics:

Diet:

Special skills:

Dragonality:

Warning:

Have you read all of the adventures
Tomas and his friends have
with the dragons?

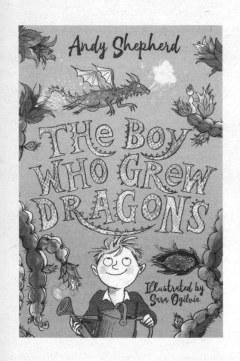

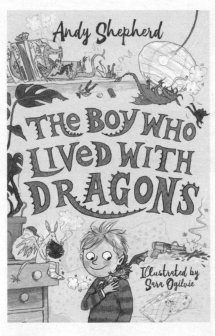

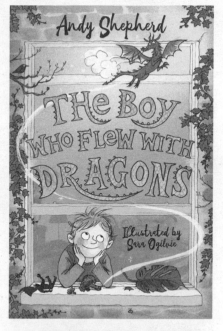

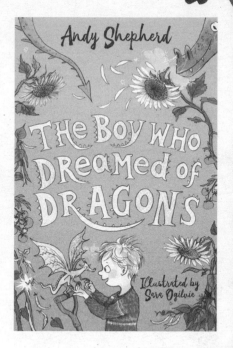

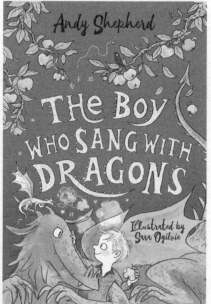

Piccadilly
PRESS

Thank you for choosing a Piccadilly Press book.

If you would like to know more about our
authors, our books or if you'd just like to know
what we're up to, you can find us online.

www.piccadillypress.co.uk

And you can also find us on:

We hope to see you soon!